Joseph Renihan

The letters of Niall the Grand

Second Edition

Joseph Renihan

The letters of Niall the Grand
Second Edition

ISBN/EAN: 9783337138011

Printed in Europe, USA, Canada, Australia, Japan

Cover: Foto ©Andreas Hilbeck / pixelio.de

More available books at **www.hansebooks.com**

THE LETTERS

OF

Niall the Grand and Others,

ON

IRISH HISTORY.

BULLS OF ADRIAN, ETC., ETC.

———:—◆—:·—

Dedicated to the Fenians and the Friends of Ireland.

————◆————

"Semper et Ubique Fideles."—Always and Everywhere Faithful.

·· — ·

SECOND EDITION--REVISED,

— ··

GRAND RAPIDS, MICH.:
STEAM PRESSES OF H. H. COLESTOCK, 2 PEARL STREET.
1882.

TABLE OF CONTENTS.

———o———

INTRODUCTORY REMARKS.

Fellow-countrymen, as myself exiles and victims of credulity and of the tyrannical policy of England and her allies, and also you men interested in the welfare of your fellow-creatures of whatever descent or nationality, I beg leave to explain to you the motives that impelled me to commence those letters of " Niall, the Grand," lately published in the DAILY DEMOCRAT, and how the ungentlemanly misconstruction of the spirit of these letters by " Irish" and " Irish-Americans " caused me, instead of treating them with neglect as they deserved, to retaliate in kind.

In my experience, I have met and talked with Irishmen who could relate with accuracy the principal incidents of English, French, Spanish, German, Russian and even Roman, Grecian, Persian and Egyptian histories, and yet knew nothing of their own country's history, except what they had learned from the erroneous fireside legends of old women, such as the counterfeit prophecies of Columkill, the great feats of fairies and ghosts, and the battles and conversations St. Patrick had with the snakes. These same men can tell you the name and merits of every story that has appeared in the NEW YORK WEEKLY, the FIRESIDE COMPANION, etc., during the last ten years. It is a desire to awaken the minds of such men to the importance of Irish history that induces me to introduce Niall. If they begin to read and study this Irish history, they will find it AS INSTRUCTIVE AS ANY OTHER, and more romantic and thrilling than the trash they find in dime novels and story papers. Despite all the pains which the Danes and their kindred, the Norman-English, took to destroy it, and the extent to which they succeeded, we can still learn from it that a people capable of leading the world in arts, science and learning may, when opposed by cunning fraud, become almost the exact opposite of what nature has made them—that circumstances move the human mind as wind does the clouds, and that the more noble and intellectual is the mind, the more subject it is to bad as well as good influence.

Countrymen, let us compare Ireland of 1,000 or 2,000 years ago with our sad and forsaken Ireland of the present, and see if the comparison flatters us. Our fathers a thousand years ago led the world in intellectual advancement, gave tuition and the necessaries and comforts of life free of charge to all that wished to partake of them; and our fathers of two thousand years ago possessed not only learning and civilization but also valor and freedom. They were not afraid to measure swords with the soldiers of doughty Rome. That power invaded and easily conquered England, the inhabitants of which the Irish, judging from their neutrality, must have thought little of; but when she attempted the subjugation of the Scotch she was met and foiled by Irish valor, and met not alone in Scotland; but, for her presumption in tampering with the rights and liberty of true Celts, encountered and defeated on her own soil. We may also congratulate ourselves on the fact that our Christian forefathers were about the only people then that practiced Christianity to the letter. They discountenanced the maxim of treating people according to desert; and alas! to the sorrow of their progeny put in rigid practice that of doing good for evil; while their neighbors believed in and practiced that and every other Christian precept as far as it enabled them to gain their selfish ends by deceiving others. Of equal truth is the fact that our forefathers, a thousand years ago, educated and civilized, so far as that was possible, the very men in the unjust possession of whose posterity Ireland is now and has been more or less for the last seven hundred years; while one-half of the rightful heirs, driven to America, have to keep the other half at home from starving; all of which we may contemplate with such emotions as are congenial to our dispositions.

"Irish" has, with other unfounded pet names, called me

a renegade Irishman. If, to be a renegade, it is necessary for one to have the welfare of his native country at heart next to that of his family and to give her all the assistance in his power, then I accept the term renegade; for Ireland is next to my family in my love and anxiety.

> Oh Erin! my country, though sad and forsaken,
> I long to revisit thy sea-beaten shore;
> But, alas! in a far foreign land I awaken,
> And sigh for the friends that can meet me no more.

If he applies the word on religious grounds, I say to him, though by no means willing to play the hypocrite, I believe myself at least as good a Catholic as he. I have nothing to say against the religious portion of Catholicity. It is the creed of every one belonging to me—the creed I was taught at the knees of a loving mother; but with that part of it that has become a political machine, to the injury of my country and its votaries, and would barter their liberty and their lives, I hold no sympathy. When a man combines in his person the character of a politician with that of an expounder and inculcator of Christian precepts and Christian virtues—that is, when he uses or rather prostitutes the influence, attached to his position as moral teacher, in gaining his own selfish object or in gratifying his vanity, to the detriment of those the faithful guardian of whose interests he pretends to be, I cannot conscientiously approve of his worldly inclination or confide in his interpretation of Christian or moral obligations.

It has been strongly urged and is now asserted that God wills to have Irishmen persecuted, stoned and exiled, so as to carry the faith to other countries! Brother Irishmen, is it your belief that God has created us for this purpose—as victims to be sacrificed to the will of a few dozen Englishmen, who use our God-given property in practicing vices for which no language has names, and so revolting that to hear them described causes one's hair to stand on end with horror! Oh! let us not commit such a blasphemy as believing such a damnable theory. If it be so, what a noble end is ours! And do we propagate the faith to any remarkable extent? Yes; the faith that Ireland has been hoodwinked more by her supposed friends than her professed enemy; and this, anyone taking the trouble of investigating the matter will find so, unless from prejudice he begins with the firm resolve to find it otherwise; but instead of converting heretics they lose their own faith and with it their patriotism, as they consider each so blended with the other and locked together in the ecclesiastical magic-box that it is impossible to retain one and discard the other. I have no conception of an institution more worthy of veneration than the Catholic Church, as a theological system; but I feel far differently toward it as a mundane concern. "Render to the Lord what is the Lord's, and to Cæsar what is Cæsar's."

When we see men, who have by vows dedicated themselves to the service of God, make the commandments of that God subservient to the tactics of a pawnbroker or a ward politician, I do not understand why we are not justified, in the eyes of God and of man, in renouncing his authority, especially the ungodly part of it, if we regard our own happiness and wish to preserve our religion from contamination. There

> "Is nought so good, but, strained from that fair use,
> Revolts from true birth, stumbling on abuse."

There must be some reason why the valor and the genius, that have triumphed so in the battles and the cause of strange lands, have met with such signal failures in Ireland. There must be some obstacle in the way; and until we have removed it, it is useless to be agitating Irish grievances, unless to keep us conscious of our degradation.

It is not expected that these remarks will remove the arbitrary despotism of Ireland's real and supposed enemies any more effectually than reverse the order of the universe; but still I consider it a duty incumbent on me to put a drop in the bucket, which I hope to God will soon be filled. I am well aware, that to be successful in trade, a man must not meddle with politics or religion, but I prefer principle to profit; hence my course in this affair. If my efforts help the cause any, I will deem myself well paid for my trouble. If otherwise, I can rest satisfied with having done what I think is my duty and what I know to be right. Sursum corda—be not disheartened. N. T. G.

LETTERS OF NIALL THE GRAND.

ST. PATRICK'S DAY.

Editors Daily Democrat:

Sirs :—It seems as if our Irish fellow-citizens are forgetting to make any preparation to celebrate the anniversary of St. Patrick. Have they come to the conclusion that there was no such person?—that the whole business was an intrigue of Rome, to annul the interests of the African church, which was then (432) established in Ireland by Peladsius? It is very true there are sixty-three histories extant on this saint, and now in the libraries of Cambridge and Oxford. Not one of the writers dare say where he was born, what country he could claim as his own, or how old he was when he died. Nor can any give any proof that he ever dreamed of Ireland or the Irish people, as is related of him in his vision (Vox Hibernijersium); or that he did actually consecrate 365 bishops—one for every day in the year—and 3,000 priests. It is light on this subject which we want. On that day to celebrate, let us have a fine concert or lecture, and send the proceeds to feed some of the poor of Ireland. A good lecture would afford instruction, and the money would help to feed the starving.

NIALL THE GRAND.

(An answer to Niall the Grand.)

ST. PATRICK'S DAY.

Editors Daily Democrat:

In reply to "Niall the Grand," I would say that "our Irish fellow-citizens" have not forgotten to consider the advisability of celebrating the 17th of March. They have

not come to the conclusion that St. Patrick never existed;
all Christians believe that he introduced the Christian religion into Ireland, even though, according to the authorities
quoted by "Niall the Grand," there may be some doubt
as to the exact date of both the birth and death of Ireland's
apostle.

With regard to the manner of celebrating the anniversary of St. Patrick, why should he suggest any fine concert, etc., until he has time to read the works of some other
historians, besides the sixty-three he mentioned; he might
then be able to let his "Irish fellow-citizens" know when
and how to celebrate. If he has any idea that his "Irish
fellow-citizens" are neglecting their duty to the land of St.
Patrick's vision (Vox Hibernijersium), I would inform him
that they forwarded nearly five hundred dollars last week,
in addition to what they had already sent to assist their
struggling brothers in Ireland, and intend to continue the
good work in spite of the sneers of the "Grand Niall." If
he has any suggestions to make with regard to the celebra-
tion he seems so anxious to take place, he can present
them either personally or by proxy, at the next meeting of
the only thorough Irish organization in this city, viz: the
Land League.   Irish American.

(Niall's Answer.)

NIALL THE GRAND.

ST. PATRICK AND THE DAY WE CELEBRATE.

Editors Daily Democrat:

The old saying is: Those whom the gods wish to destroy,
they first make mad. My suggestion, as to the apparent
negligence of our Irish fellow-citizens, was in the most
friendly spirit. Still, I am charged with sneering at the
day we are going to celebrate. Are we to wait and consult
my friend "Irish-American," before we venture to men-
tion or question the powers that be? Oh ye gods! my
letter made no reference to that good organization, the land

league, the members of which it is an honor to be
acquainted with; still, I do not like to see them boasting of
their charity. Did "Irish-American" contribute $5 to it?
I think not. But to return to St. Patrick: The reader
will see your correspondent only believes like the rest; and
so, without knowing, he is happy in the delusion. I think
there is not another country on the face of the earth that
has had more of this religion preached to them and profited
less. Let me draw your attention to a few facts: The
missionaries of the third century not only preached but
founded churches and colleges in Ireland. Among the
names of these men are Holy Diana, Heber, founder of an
academy at Big-lire in Leinster. St. Kieran and St. Declan
also preceded St. Patrick, and founded churches. Ibarris
protested against giving the supremacy and patronage of
Ireland to anyone but a native. Enough! St. Patrick did
not introduce Christianity into Ireland. But let us see how
much social happiness Ireland has enjoyed since her connection with Rome. Ireland was free and happy. It was
a land of milk and honey before her connection with that
power. But in the 348 years between the arrival of St.
Patrick and the Danish invasion (770) what had occurred?
When the Danes came, the Irish did not know how to
defend themselves from a handful of pirates, allowing them
to destroy the colleges and churches, and so absorbed in
religion were we that we did not know the use of arms.
We suffered the most galling and degrading slavery.

Do you forget the nose-tax, in default of the money tribute, to be paid to the Danes? Oh yes; why were not the
Irish of that date united? I will save you the mortifica-
tion; they paid too much attention to the mandates of
Rome.

But if "Irish-American" will give a little more attention
to the history of Ireland, he will see that the church is
partly responsible for Ireland's slavery. Let me draw his
attention to the bulls which were issued at different times
from Rome; for instance, Adrian IV. to Henry II. When
Bruce led the Scottish and Irish army, the pope lent his

aid to the English; for we see O'Neill, Prince of Tyrone, making the following remonstrance, in the year 1318: "It is with difficulty we can bring ourselves to believe that the biting and venomous calumnies, with which we and all who espouse our cause have been invariably assailed by the English, should have found admittance also into the mind of your holiness." [O'Halloran, p. 50, second div., chapter 9; J. Frost, vol. 2, page 281.] Speaking of the conquest of Ireland by Henry, having obtained a papal bull, etc., Sherlock (page 33) says Pope Adrian granted a license to Henry to invade and convert Ireland. Is it not time that Irishmen should be honest enough to lay the cause of their misery where it properly belongs? I hold our present state of slavery is as much to be charged to the church-men as to the English; and until Irishmen realize the fact, it is the honest conviction of your correspondent that this will continue.

With many thanks for your valuable space, I remain yours,   NIALL THE GRAND.

"IRISH" VS. "NIALL THE GRAND."

ANOTHER CORRESPONDENT TAKES A HAND IN THE GAME.

Grand Rapids, Feb. 24, 1882.

EDITORS DAILY DEMOCRAT:

Sirs:—Will you please permit me to say, for the gratifi-cation of this newly-fledged genius, "Niall the Grand," who has been figuring in the Democrat within the past few days, how thankful, oh! how very thankful the Irish people of Grand Rapids are for his noble conduct in thus demonstrating to them the wickedness of their ways by wilfully remaining in ignorance. And yet, look at the per-versity of those victims of Rome; for a great many of them have the ingratitude to say to their would-be benefac-tor that the proffered advice smells badly. And yet more wicked, they say it is rather late in this, the nineteenth century. to pay any attention to the ranting tirade of this most illustrious authority, who tells them that when "the

Danes came, the Irish were not able to defend themselves
from a handful of pirates." Well, for once, we will be
honest, and say we were not able to defend ourselves; and
why? Not, as the great Niall would imply, but because
there were then, as now, traitors and renegades, who professed to be our friends, ready and willing to do the dirty
work of our enemies. More " wickedness " still; for they
add that there are some of the posterity of those same
traitors and knaves in Grand Rapids to-day. " Most noble
Niall." I pity you, after such abnegation, self-sacrifice and
trouble on your part, to be subject to such treatment from
such " Rome-ridden slaves " as you say the Irish are.

And a word in conclusion. It is the opinion of a number of people, in this city, that the sooner you take your
exit out of the public view as a historian and lecturer of
the Irish people the better; for it is proved beyond a
doubt, by your own quotation of history, that either you or
history—perhaps both—are wrong. So that, before you
take to yourself the liberty of correcting " Irish-American,"
you ought to become more authentic yourself. You say
that Henry obtained a papal bull or license to invade and
convert Ireland, from Pope Adrian. Now, it has been
proved, beyond the shadow of a doubt, that Henry never
attempted to establish that he had received such authority
till long after the pope's death, and why? Because such
authority never existed.

And now, permit me to add that, as the Irish people
have long since formed their opinion in regard to their
religion and country, and as they are said to be a perverse
people, it will take a more learned and logical authority
than the celebrated Niall the Grand to change them; for I
think he might be reasonably suspected of being a traducer
of both. I am sir, etc.,   IRISH.

"NIALL THE GRAND AGAIN."

HE REPLIES PROMPTLY TO THE STRICTURES OF "IRISH."

Grand Rapids, February 25.

EDITORS DAILY DEMOCRAT:

Sirs :—Niall the Grand has received another shot from "Irish." "Irish-American" is hors de combat. Now I have only to deal with ignorant "Irish." I say ignorant, because he has not proven me wrong ; nor did he have the intelligence to make any argument to contradict one single assertion of Niall the Grand. He is, like a great many, satisfied if a priest or Catholic writer denies anything ; it must be so. I thank him for his advice to leave the lecture and historical field; but before I drop this subject I will teach him more than he ever knew. You will notice, he makes the bold assertion that Henry the Second did not receive a bull from Pope Adrian, the spurious son of a fallen priest, and a beggar [Lives of the Popes] ; a scholar by charity, educated by Maurice O'Garman, a professor in Paris. Irish does not believe in this bull of Adrian. Oh no ! My authorities are G. Cambensis chaplain to Henry, Dr. Leland, Dr. O'Connor, O'Halloran and T. Moore. But to make sure—doubly sure—here is Pope Alexander the Third's bull, which will speak for itself, and confirms Adrian's bull, and is as follows :

" Alexander, bishop, servant of the servants of God, to his dear son in Christ, the illustrious king of England, health and apostolical benediction :

" Forasmuch as these things, which have been on good reasons granted by our predecessors, deserve to be confirmed in the fullest manner ; and considering the grant of the dominion of the realm of Ireland by the venerable Pope Adrian, we, pursuing his footsteps, do ratify and confirm the same, (reserving to St. Peter and to the holy Roman church, as well in England as in Ireland, the yearly pension of one penny from every house) provided that the abominations of the land being removed, that barbarous people, Christians only in name, may, by your means, be reformed, and their lives and conversation mended, so that their disordered church being thus reduced to regular discipline, that nation may, with the name of Christians, be so in act and deed. Given at Rome in the year of salvation 1172."

How much it restrained the hands of the Irish, not only upon this, but upon future occasions, we may infer from the following remarkable words in a memorial from O'Neil, king of Ulster, presented in 1330 to John XXII, pope of Rome, in the name of the Irish people:

"During the course of so many ages (three thousand years), our sovereigns preserved the independence of their country. Attacked more than once by foreign powers, they wanted neither force nor courage to repel the bold invaders; but that which they dared do against force, they could not against the simple decree of your predecessors." Adrian, etc.

I quote the following from John Q. Adams' address in the American House of Representatives, in 1845–6: "The pope was in the custom of giving away not only all barbarous countries, with their inhabitants, but at times civilized countries too. He dethroned sovereigns, laid their kingdoms under interdict, and excommunicated them; and all this was submitted to. And the government of Great Britain, at this day, holds Ireland by no other title. Three hundred years before the grant of America to Ferdinand and Isabella, Pope Adrian gave Ireland to Henry the Second of England; and England holds the island by that title now, unless indeed she sets up another title by conquest; but Ireland, if in form conquered, has been in almost perpetual rebellion ever since. England has been obliged to reconquer her some half-dozen times; and if she means to do it now, she must begin soon. The question has been raised whether Ireland shall be independent, and if we get into a war, it will be a pretty serious matter for England to maintain her title." We find a bull against the British, in favor of William the Conqueror, in 1066; one in 1311; and a bull of Pope Lucius in favor of John Cumming, who was elected archbishop of Dublin in 1180. [O'Halloran, a Roman Catholic writer, 2d Div., page 83.)

Oh, Mr. Editor, I am full of those Irish bulls. I have another shot at "Irish." I hope to destroy his mean bigotry. I will hand you the black list of Irish bishops, priests and laymen, names very common in our city directory, as you will see; not one of the name of your correspondent is to be found in the infamous record. I will also give you the names of the traitors from FitzPatrick of Ossory, 1014, to Bishop Moriarity of Kerry.

In conclusion, Mr. Editor, I am still asking, as I did in my first letter, will some one who knows, tell me if St. Patrick ever lived? The learned Doctor Ledwich, in his Antiquities of Ireland, says he did not live. Let us have light on the subject.

NIALL THE GRAND.

"IRISH" VS. "NIALL THE GRAND."

MORE ABOUT THE BOGUS BULL OF POPE ADRIAN.

Grand Rapids, Feb. 27, 1822.

EDITORS DAILY DEMOCRAT:

Sirs:—In reply to the latest scurrilous production of Niall the Grand, I would beg to say that only for the shameful and deliberate misstatements put forward, I would consider such "billingsgate" beneath notice. He says he has received another shot from "ignorant Irish." Most noble victim! When Irish shoots, he prefers shooting at something besides a shadow. Again he tells me, that before he is done with this matter that he will teach me more than ever I knew. Halt, Niall! you have done so already; for you have proved beyond doubt that no falsehood is too glaring, no mire too filthy for a renegade Irishman to indulge and crawl in.

But to come to the point, behold the virtuous surprise of the august Niall at my denying the bull, which it is alleged Henry received from Pope Adrian. I would here remark,

with regard to the foul-mouthed calumny of this model
writer in reference to the holy pontiff, that the assertion is
as false as the audacity and malignity of Niall the Grand
which make it ; for I defy him to point it out in the Lives
of the Popes. But to return again, I do deny it, and have
the best authority for doing so. And here let me draw the
attention of the reader to the vacillating nature of this
wonderful writer. First, he proposed proving the authenticity of the original bull. Does he do so? No; but he
comes out with a flourish, and quotes one alleged to have
been obtained years afterward, and from a different source.
But more of that anon.

Now, if the most learned Niall has read all the history
which he says he has, he should have been in a position to
give the date of this famous document. But no; he don't.
nor neither do any of the celebrated authorities which he
gives us. No, Niall, neither does any one historian ; and
why? For the very good reason that there never was any
date to it. However, Francis Page, Rymer and others
allege it was obtained in 1154; but this is incorrect, for
Henry was crowned December 19th, 1154, and conse-
quently could not have received it in that year. Of course
I do not deny that a document of the kind did exist. What
I do deny is the genuineness of it ; and I will give him my
authority bye and bye. In the first place, as I remarked,
the bull was never dated ; again, if Henry was so anxious
to obtain it, in order to obtain Ireland, it is singular that he
should wait till long after the pope's death to present his
credentials to the Irish people. Yet it is alleged that this
precious epistle was obtained in 1154, and it never saw the
light of day till 1174, and it was only when his (Henry's)
authority was annihilated in Ireland, when this "hidden
treasure" was held up to the gaze of the "ignorant Irish."
So, so, Niall.

Now, will you condescend to listen to what McGeoghey-
an's and Mitchell's "Ireland" say? "In truth, were we
to consider the circumstances and motives of the bull, it
has the appearance of a fictitious one." (Page 246). More

authority, Niall; just listen to what the same says of this same bull, and the one which you intend should demolish "ignorant Irish :" "These bulls have all the appearance of forgery. They are not to be met with in any collection. It appears, also, that Henry II. considered them so insufficient to strengthen his dominion in Ireland that he solicited Pope Lucius III., who succeeded Alexander, to confirm them ; but that pope was too just to authorize his usurpation, and paid no attention to a considerable sum of money sent him." Page 250.

Now, I would direct the attention of the reader to the absurdity of "Niall the Grand," in the first place asking the Irishmen of Grand Rapids to celebrate the feast of St. Patrick, and in the same breath ask "Irish-American" or "ignorant Irish" to prove that there was such a man. Now the idea is so foolish that "Niall" might just as well ask me to prove that one and one make two, or that there were such places as America or Ireland. There is not a man in Ireland but believes it ; and unless I am much mistaken, there was a day when the skeptical Niall the Grand believed so too, but as for the change. If that is not enough, we have tradition handing it down to us. Yes ; and we have the Catholic church, the oldest and most reliable historian to all. She celebrates a feast in his honor. Again, we have her bishops and priests who read a special office in the mass of that day. What a lot of fools all those learned men must be to be practicing devotion in honor of a saint who never existed ! Niall says he did not ; but Usher, Ware, Colgan, Dr. Lanegan and the Four Masters say he did. I leave to the public to judge whether Niall the Grand or they are the best authority.

Now, in conclusion, this mighty Niall tells us because we are bound to Rome, we are and will be slaves so long as we keep up the connection. Most glorious Niall! what a wonderful prophet you are ! You seem to forget our history began with Christianity ; our glories were all intertwined with our religion ; our national banner was inscribed with the emblem of faith, " the green immortal shamrock."

The brightest names in our history were all associated with our religion—Malachi dying in the midst of the monks, and clothed with their holy habit; Brian "the great king," upholding the crucifix before his army on the morning of Clontarf, and expiring in its embraces before sunset. All those would Niall have us forget and become recreant to, like himself.

Pardon me, Mr. Editor; I've trespassed too much; I shall not trouble you again. And as I now take leave of this modern luminary, Niall, I'll quote for him an adage from one of the old classic writers, which says: "Let the cobbler stick to his last and the tailor to his goose." That this is appropriate in the present case is the opinion of

Yours sincerely,   IRISH.

A NEW HAND AT THE BELLOWS.

J. R. REVIEWS "NIALL THE GRAND," "IRISH" AND "IRISH-AMERICAN."

EDITORS DAILY DEMOCRAT:

Sirs: In your issues of the 21st, 23d, 25th, and 26th, there appeared communications under the different nom de plumes of "Niall the Grand," "Irish-American" and "Irish." These gentlemen seem to think all they have said and written on the subject is the end; and that we must perfect our happiness by creating disunion and doubt. All Christendom believes the early writers mentioned; and even the authorities of Niall the Grand are all sufficient to prove that St. Patrick was the second bishop sent from Rome as primate to Ireland. [Usher's Church Hist., chap. 16, p. 800.]

Protestant and Catholic alike look with contempt on any one who wants to destroy the faith and nationality of the people. A free manly discussion of any question relating to religion or one's history should be above meanness;

men should not forget that they owe it to their neighbors
to be dignified in talking, writing and dealing with their
fellow-men. I hope I will satisfy Niall the Grand that Ireland not only had one St. Patrick but two.

The principal authors of the life of St. Patrick are Saint
Secudinus or Seaghin, bishop of Domack Sechmald, new
Donseachlin, in Meath ; he was a disciple of the saint, and
his nephew by his sister Darerca, and composed hymns in
honor of his master, which may be seen in Colgan.

St. Loman, his disciple, and nephew by his sister Figrid,
Bishop of Athrum, now Tim, in Meath ; St. Mel, bishop of
Ordach, his disciple and nephew ; also, brother of St.
Secundinus ; and a second St. Patrick, to whom the saint
gave his own name, holding him over the baptismal font ;
all three wrote the acts of his life. The last, after the death
of his uncle, retired to the abbey of Glastonbury in Somer-
setshire in England, where he ended his days.

Saint Benignus, who succeeded St. Patrick in the see of
Ardmach, is reckoned among the authors of his life.

These four lives, says Jocelin, were written partly in Irish
and partly in Latin, by his four disciples. St. Benignus, his
successor, St. Mel and St. Loman, bishops, and St. Patrick,
his godson." [Mitchell's History of Ireland, part 2d, chap.
9, page 141.]

St. Patrick, according to Usher, was a native of North
Britain. He was born at a place now called Kirkpatrick,
not far from the city of Glasgow, in the year A. D. 372.
[Fitzgerald's History of Limerick, vol. 1, page 124.]

I will refer my friend Niall the Grand to Gidas, a disciple of St. Patrick, and one of the most ancient British historians, who is said to have presided over the college of
Arnaugh, founded by St. Patrick. Among its students
were Swithbert, the apostle of Westphalia; Willibrod, archbishop of Utrecht ; Zeargall, the philosopher and mathe-
matician known as Virgil. Even Doctor Ledwich, quoted
by Niall, expresses his astonishment at the advances learning had made in Ireland in the fifth and sixth centuries.

Oh! dear Niall, there are two sides to history. I prefer to look at the brightest side. I hope you will give us something which will please and instruct—something that will unite us in the love of religion and nationality. As you are aware, disunity is and has been the curse of our race. Devote your historical knowledge to picturing Ireland in the days of her greatness; cement together all who would fall away in doubt. We have a grand record—a proud history older than the Gospel. If our people in the hour of temptation faltered, you must remember the words of our Lord, "Forgive them father; they know not what they do." "Irish-American," stop your scribbling. Go on with the good work of helping the good Christian man, Parnell, in his noble work. "Irish," I am sure, will ever be found to protect what is right. Never will a true Irishman forget the land of learning. What land can look at such a bright past in all her gloom and in all her confusion? She has given to the world men and women who adorned every walk in life, and add new lustre to our religion and country.

> Readers, this year, it grieves my heart to tell,
> In battle three relations nobly fell,
> Fighting for king, religion, country, laws—
> Angels and men approve the glorious cause;
> Their mangled sides exhibiting to view
> The Virgin's white, the Martyr's purple hue.
> Well may the herald's emblematic lore
> Their bright achievments blazon o'er and o'er
> With dew-dropt lillies in a purple stream;
> Marble, immortalize each hero's name.
>
> J. R.

NIALL VS. IRISH.

ANOTHER RED-HOT BLAST ON THE "BOGUS" BULL BUSINESS.

March 1, 1882.

EDITORS DAILY DEMOCRAT:

Sirs:—In yours, of this morning's issue, appears the last of the correspondent "Irish." The lying fool did not give one single authority in contradiction of those "bogus" bulls in question. It is very evident he is mad, because he can not write in the spirit of his Irish Christianity. It wants another St. Patrick to convert this champion of the church. He as well as Niall knows the bull in question was issued in 1156; but he has not the spirit of truth or honor to say so. Oh! "Mr. Irish!" give us something worthy of your race; and, if the heavens fall, truth will still prevail. Your heart says you should speak the truth; but your cowardly tongue will flip. Oh! what a fallen thing a man is, when he for any consideration barters away his manhood to the powers that be! He quotes MacGeoghegan. Now that MacGeoghegan was a priest; and he, knowing full well that those bulls would come in judgment and confound the people of Ireland, casts some doubts intentionally on them.

Irish charges me with being foul-mouthed with audacity, malignity, calumny and illogicalness. I could say the same of him; but I do not want to use such language to any man, when expressing his opinion, even if he be in error.

I now draw his attention to the falsity of his charges against me; and I will accept his challenge to prove the truthfulness of my statement in reference to Adrian. Irish, your attention is called to the following, from S. O. Halloran's History of Ireland. O'Halloran was a Catholic writer; and he states, in book XIII., chap. 3d, page 307,

"The validity of these bulls, I think, cannot be doubted; it only remains to know how they were procured, and why bulls granted at such distances from each other, and for the same purpose, should appear at one and the same time?"

"This investigation will be at the same time a refutation of the argument offered against them. Adrian was by birth an Englishman—the spurious offspring of a priest. Deserted by his father, he repaired to Paris, and was there instructed in philosophy and divinity by Marianus O'Gorman, professor of the seven liberal sciences (so he is styled) as he himself acknowledges. In 1154 he was raised to the pontificate; and some time after Henry II. was proclaimed

king of England, he sent a formal embassy to congratulate
the new pope on his elevation. This mark of attention
in Henry was highly pleasing to Adrian. A strict friend-
ship arose between them ; and this encouraged the young
king, whose ambition was boundless, to request a grant of
the kingdom of Ireland from the pope. It was a flattering
circumstance to him as pontiff, as it was acknowledging the
power, assumed by the see of Rome, of disposing of kingdoms and empires. He, by this means, gratified the desire
of aggrandizing his native country, added a fresh accession
of wealth and power to Rome, and rendered a mighty
prince one of her tributaries."

"Such were the reasons that prevailed on Adrian to
grant the kingdom of Ireland to Henry."

And now, as to Adrian being a beggar, I draw Irish's
attention to the Lives of the Popes, approved by all bishops and priests, page 95. [Walsh's Ecclesiastical History.]

"Nicholas Breakspear was born at Abbot Langley, in
Hertfordshire, England. He was the son of a beggar, and
lived on Alms from the convent of St. Ruf, near Avignon."

Niall not only quotes from authority to prove beyond a
doubt ; but now he will draw on his reserve and satisfy
"Irish." Father Lavalle, in his "Brian Boroimme, the
Younger," page 23, says—

"The republication of the bull granted by the pope made
a great impression on the minds of the Irish, who, accus-
tomed to a blind obedience to every mandate from Rome,
refused on several occasions to fight the English, and even
surrendered their arms at the orders of Cardinal Vivian,
the pope's legate, who forbade them, under pain of excommunication to use them against the English."

Will "Irish" ask himself how it came to pass that the
MacArthy, of Desmond, was the first of the Munster
princes who swore fealty to the English monarch. Then
Donald, king of Thermond, and the prince of Ossory and
Decies. How will "Irish" explain away the synod of
Cashel, which was splendid and numerous. Besides the

legate, there appeared the archbishops of Munster, Leinster and Connaught, with their suffragans, and many abbots and inferior clergy.

The bull of Adrian IV. was then produced.

I now say that 1,773 men under Strongbow, Fitzgerald and Fitzmaurice could not have conquered Ireland with the help of the traitor, MacMurchad.

Is there an Irishman living who will say the small English army could have conquered Ireland if they had not been armed with these bulls of Adrian and Alexander. More authority—Fleury, Ecclesiastical History, tome XV., p. 423 ; O'Halloran, p. 308.

Alexander confirmed the donation of Adrian, in consequence of a request from the Irish clergy.

The bishop and clergy of Wexford ordered the surrender of the town to the British, to stop the effusion of Christian blood. Has the church anything to do with this Irish slavery. That she had is proven beyond a doubt, except to such as my friend "Irish."

Christian, bishop of Lismore, who had been for some time a Christian monk in the abbey of Clairvalle, under St. Bernard, was now constituted the pope's legate in Ireland, and in that capacity he presided at a synod held in the abbey of Mellifont in 1157.

Mortogh IV., monarch of Ireland, with many of the Irish princes, attended this assembly, at which Dunchad O'Melaghlin, king of Meath, was excommunicated and deposed, and his territories given to his brother Dermond.

The union of the Irish church with that of Rome seems now to have been completed ; for we find that, on the death of Gregory, Archbishop of Dublin, his successor, Lawrence O'Toole, was consecrated in Ireland ; for, before this, they as well as the prelates of Waterford and Limerick, as already hinted at, received their consecration from the archbishop of Canterbury.

One of the first objects of Henry II., after his arrival in this country was to obtain the sanction of the Irish clergy to his ambitious designs.

For this purpose, a synod was convened in his name, which assembled in Cashel in 1172, Christian, bishop of Lismore, the pope's legate, presiding upon that occasion.

Several of the English clergy attended, on the part of Henry, and Brompton, abbot of Jerval in Yorkshire, informs us that the king received from every archbishop and bishop charters with their seals pendant, whereby they constituted him and his heirs kings and lords of Ireland forever; to which Roger Hoveden adds that the king sent a transcript of these charters to Pope Alexander, who by his apostolic authority confirmed the kingdom to him and his heirs.

Leland, however, expresses some doubt whether this was a general assembly of the clergy, adding that the Primate Gelasius certainly did not attend, excusing himself on account of age and infirmities; and that the prelates of Ulster followed the example of their metropolitan; but Giraldus Cambrensis, in opposition to the Irish annalists, asserts that Gelasius came to Dublin soon after, and gave his full assent to the transactions and ordinances of this synod. The proposed design of the king, in convening this assembly, was to fulfill the wishes of Pope Adrian, as expressed in his bull. [Fitzgerald's Irish Antiquities, page 142.]

Mr. Editor, I am now prepared to clip a little of "J. R." in my next. I hope he will prove himself better metal, more truthful and manly at least, and say something to instruct. In my next, I propose to give the cause of the quarrel between Henry, Becket and Adrian, all Englishmen, the feast of Easter, and the Independence of the old Irish church for five hundred years. From 494 to 994, Ireland had no connection with Rome.

NIALL THE GRAND.

"TYRO" TAKES A HAND.

HE REVIEWS "NIALL THE GRAND," "IRISH" AND "IRISH-AMERICAN."

Grand, Rapids, March 3, 1882.

EDITORS DAILY DEMOCRAT:

Sirs:—It is not at all gratifying to men of Irish or any

other nationality, to see the manner in which "Niall the
Grand," "Irish" and "Irish-American" are carrying on
their discussion. If I understand Niall correctly, what he
wishes to demonstrate to us, and firmly believes himself is,
first, that the close connection which the popes of Rome
maintain should exist between the spiritual and temporal
authorities is detrimental to the advancement of harmony
and happiness, in Ireland particularly; and has been a
stumbling block to Irish freedom and felicity for the last
seven hundred years; and secondly, that St. Patrick is a
myth. What the object of "Irish" is, I wish himself
would inform us.

I sincerely agree with Niall, if he holds that religion and
politics, bringing into consideration the many different
shades of religious belief, should be practiced and admin-
istered separately, and that a total separation of the two
would be advantageous to each, and conducive to general
good feeling. That the Roman Catholic church has been
directly or indirectly the cause of nearly if not quite all
the English-inflicted misery of Ireland, since the time of
Pope Adrian the Fourth, can hardly be questioned by any
man giving the subject anything like due and impartial
investigation. That never-to-be-forgotten bull of pope
Adrian to Henry the Second of England, authorizing that
king to plunder Ireland, has caused much superfluous discussion. Our forefathers saw the effect it had produced;
and we need not wonder that they were imposed upon as
they were—were willing to believe Adrian or any pope of
Rome incapable of committing so grievous a crime. However, there have always been in Ireland those who would
have shuddered at the thought of such an act, had there
appeared to them the least improbability of the authenticity of the bull that admitted Adrian's grant of Ireland to
England. None will, I think, doubt the erudition of T. D.
McGee; and he freely admits that Adrian presented Henry
with the document in question. The celebrated Catholic
historian, Dr. Lingard, whose only incentive here could
have been the love of truth, speaks thus of the matter:

" To justify the invasion of a free and unoffending people,
his (Henry's) ambition had discovered that the civilization
of their manners and the reform of their clergy were benefits which the Irish ought cheerfully to purchase with the
loss of their independence. Within a few months after his
coronation, John of Salisbury, a learned monk, was dis-
patched to solicit the approbation of Pope Adrian. The
envoy was charged to assure his holiness that Henry's
principal object was to provide instruction for an ignorant
people, to extirpate vice from the Lord's vineyard, and to
extend to Ireland the annual payment of Peter-pence; but
that, as every Christian island was the property of the holy
see, he did not presume to make the attempt without the
advice and consent of the successor of St. Peter. The
pontiff, who must have smiled at the hypocrisy of this
address, praised in his reply the piety of his dutiful son ;
accepted and asserted the right of sovereignty which had
been so liberally admitted ; expressed the satisfaction with
which he assented to the king's request ; and exhorted him
to bear always in mind the conditions on which that assent
had been grounded." I quote Lingard before all others,
because he is acknowledged by the strictest of Catholics as
a historian of undoubted veracity and ability, and not at
all likely to confirm an indelible stain on the character of
Pope Adrian, his own countryman, for the mere love of
falsehood—Adrian, too, being head of the church of which
Lingard professed himself a sincere votary and devout
priest. It is very probable that Adrian did not foresee,
when he granted Henry permission to " civilize " Ireland,
any abuse of the conditions on which that permission was
given ; for politics was not his forte any more than that of
other ecclesiastics. Adrian's conditional gift of Ireland to
England must be considered the first and greatest of an
indefinite series of ecclesistical burdens imposed on that
credulous island. Every clerical interference in temporal
affairs since that has proved a most bitter curse to it and
its freedom, and cost thousands of Irish money and shed
hogsheads of English as well as Irish blood. There seems

to be a fatality attached to all priestly dabbling in politics.
The meddling of even the patriotic and holy O"Toole went
hand in hand with disaster. It is admitted by all, except
those whom it most concerns, that the pretensions of Rome
to superiority in matters temporal as well as spiritual, in
Ireland, were the principal weapons wielded by the soldiers
and the undertakers, since the introduction thither of the
reformation. And the reasons why non-Catholics there to-
day are so unanimously English in legislative ideas is, as
they say and believe, because home-rule means Rome-rule.

Seeing that politics and religion are so different in nature,
and that an inseparable union of them is equally imcom-
patible with the best interests of each, it is a complete
mystery to a great many outside the priesthood why the
Catholic church insists so inveterately on continuing the
union and on making one a mere tool for the other. An
object of Christ was to promote the general welfare of the
human family, and to ameliorate the condition of every
living creature, if we are to judge from his principal commandment, "Love your neighbor as yourself," or "Do
unto others as you would have others do unto you." He
and His Father would not certainly ordain that we should
waste time and labor building churches and attending services solely for the pleasure of seeing us do so, as some of
us, on a cold day, would glory in witnessing a dog swim for
a stick wantonly thrown into the river. The philanthropic
prop of Christianity is what supports it with such firmness,
and not the sword and gibbet. Whether right or wrong, a
great many Catholics and non-Catholics are strongly im-
pressed with the belief that "love one another" is the
essential commandment, and that all others are only trib-
ntary to it.

This is my faith, and I think something like the faith of
Niall the Grand too; and I believe also that the order or
institution that wilfully retards human happiness, or even
the comfort of the brute, is not indifferently Christian, but
a perfect demon in the full meaning of that word. To wind
up this matter, I will say that while Ireland gratefully

accepts the alternate slaps of Rome and England, as she does at present, she will be what she is.

What object Niall has in asserting that St. Patrick is a myth is something too hard for me to penetrate. St. Patrick is said to have brought no army with him to scourge the inhabitants, and no weapons but good will toward man, and the salutary precepts of Christianity; and, so far as I can judge, the simple doctrine introduced by him into Ireland was far from being the complex unintelligible concern, that some forms of Christianity to-day are. St. Patrick is believed by a large majority of our learned men to have lived and taught in Ireland, and to have been one of the most amiable of men. What then induces Niall, to doubt his having existed? "J. R." indulges in the opposite extreme, and affirms that there were two or three St. Patricks. Bravo! J. R.; the more the better. Still, if it is all the same to J. R. and Niall, it would be highly pleasing to quite a few Irishmen if they compromise the matter and give us, for keeps, one respectable St. Patrick, in drinking to whose memory, next 17th, we can for a short time drown our sorrows.

It is to be hoped, that, hereafter Nial the Grand and Irish will take a more courteous mode of settling their grievances than applying to each other such adjectives as " scurrilous," " ignorant," etc.

By giving the above insertion in your valuable paper, you will confer a favor on a number of your readers. Thankfully yours,   TYRO.

ARTFUL POLICY OF THE ENGLISH GOVERNMENT.

It has been the policy of the English government, whenever it meditated any great wrong against the Irish people, to employ, first of all, some pliant priest to do the preparatory work. This was the trick of Henry II. No sooner had that monarch laid an evil eye, on Ireland, than he communicated his design to Giraldus Cambrensis, a priest;

and this Giraldus Cambrensis, at the express command of his royal master, immediately set to work to write a "History of Ireland," a book full of lies from cover to cover. In this "history of Ireland," the Irish are described as a savage, murderous and irreligious people. Transcripts of the book were made, and sent all over Europe. The book was sent to Rome also. The aim of Henry II. was apparent. It was to create an opinion unfavorable to the good name of the Irish, so that when he should undertake his invading enterprise, the act would find some show of palliation. Listen to what Abbe Geoghegan (History of Ireland, p. 18,) says :

A PRIEST IN THE ENGLISH INTEREST WRITES A LYING HISTORY OF IRELAND, IN ORDER TO FURTHER ENGLISH INTRIGUE AT ROME.

" Gerald Barry, a priest, and native of the country of Wales, in England, called Cambria in Latin, (from whence is derived the name of Cambrensis, under which he is known,) was the first stranger who undertook to write the history of Ireland, in order to perpetuate the calumnies which his countrymen had already published against its inhabitants. Circumstances required that they should make the Irish pass for barbarians. The title of Henry the Second to Ireland was founded only upon a bull obtained clandestinely from Pope Adrian the Fourth, an Englishman by birth. The cause of this bull was a false statement, which Henry had given to the Pope, of the impiety and barbarism of the Irish nation. Cambrensis was then ordered to verify, by writing, the statement upon which the granting of the bull had been extorted. He did not fail to intermix his work with calumnies and groundless absurdities. However, the credit of a powerful king knew how to make even the court of Rome believe them. It was in this spirit that Cambrensis wrote his history; and from thence the English authors have taken the false coloring under which ancient Ireland has been represented."

Here we find that the first man who wrote a history of Ireland in the English interest—the first model and prototype of Froude in our day—was a priest. The first agent,

too, employed by the British Government, at Rome, in the
English interest, and against Ireland, was a priest. His
name is John of Salisbury. Here is what the nun of Kenmare, in her history of Ireland, (p. 274,) says of the transaction:

AN ENGLISH PRIEST IS SENT TO ROME, TO ASK IRELAND OF THE
POPE, AS A GIFT FOR THE KING OF ENGLAND.

"It has been already shown that the possession of Ireland was coveted, at an early period, by the Norman rulers
of Great Britain. When Henry II. ascended the throne in
1154, he probably intended to take the matter in hands at
once. An Englishman, Adrian IV., filled the papal chair.
The English monarch would naturally find him favorable
to his own country. John of Salisbury, then chaplain to
the Archbishop of Canterbury, was commissioned to
request the favor. No doubt he represented his master as
very zealous for the interests of religion, and made it appear that his sole motive was the good, temporal and
spiritual, of the barbarous Irish. At least, this is plainly
implied in Adrian's bull."

We have pointed out these two unscrupulous priests
working in the English interest. Were they unscrupulous
because they were priests? Certainly not. But it is because they were priests—men wearing the cloak of religion—that Henry II. deemed them the fittest instruments to
employ in furthering his unscrupulous design.

Some one, perhaps, will tell us that this bull of Adrian
IV. is a forgery. Its authenticity has been denied by some
few ecclesiastical orators of late; but denial is not disproof.
Be this as it may, however, the plottings of the English
king against the rights and liberties of the Irish people—
and the iniquitous service rendered him by his English
priests—are indisputable. But the bull itself cannot be
questioned. The story itself has the elements of proba-
bility. It is undeniable that the power of taking away the
government of a country from one man and giving it to
another man was claimed and exercised by the pope in

that age. It is shown that Henry II. sought to influence Rome in his behalf, in this transaction; and it is he that based his claim on the bull of Adrian IV. [Nun of Kenmare's History of Ireland.]

IRISHMEN! LOOK AND READ FOR YOURSELVES!

MAYNOOTH COLLEGE ENDOWED BY ENGLAND.

The American revolution closed. Then arose the French revolution. This latter revolution was an uprising against the power of the aristocracy, and England—the most aristocratic nation in the world—trembled at the prospect. She feared these French revolutionists would stir up the Irish; and so they did. Wolfe Tone, Napper Tandy, Lord Edward Fitzgerald, with others, had put themselves in communication with the French leaders, and were now active in organizing an insurrection in Ireland. With this danger staring them in the face, the astute statesmen of England, abandoning their former policy of hostility to the Catholic church, began to make friendly overtures to the Irish priests. Said these statesmen to the Irish bishops: "Why have you not a college in Ireland for the training of priests? It doesn't look well to see ecclesiastical students go to France for their education. That's a bad country, you know, for young Irishmen." So, in 1795, Maynooth College was founded. It received a government grant of $40,000 a year. After a while the government grant was raised to $150,000 a year, not to speak of $300,000 expended by government, from time to time, by way of repairs on the college. This appears very generous in the British government; but the generous British government knew right well what it was driving at. Speaking of this Maynooth business, Sister Clare (History of Ireland, p. 111,) says:

THE MAYNOOTH GRANT A BRIBE FROM THE ENGLISH GOVERNMENT TO LOYALIZE THE IRISH PRIESTS.

"As the government had some apprehensions lest the

Catholics should avenge themselves in any way for the duplicity with which they had been treated [in the rejection of the Catholic claims] it was proposed to establish the College of Maynooth. The excuse to those who objected to granting even the least favor to Catholics, had the advantages of being a plausible one. It was said that being educated abroad tended to render them [the priests] disloyal; and certainly to deny a man's education in his own country, and oblige him to endure the labor and expense of expatriation in order to obtain it, was not naturally the best method of inducing affection for the power which compelled this course. It was, moreover, believed that if government endowed Maynooth, the Irish hierarchy would feel bound in return to support the government. It was at least certain to all but the most obtuse, that a rebellion was imminent in Ireland; and this seemed a probable means of enlisting the Catholic clergy on the side of England."

It was not to advance the Catholic faith, but to crush Irish nationality, that the British government gave its aid and support to Maynooth College. This is unquestionable. One hundred and fifty thousand dollars a year is a big sum; but England didn't give away this big sum for nothing. It was advance payment for loyal services to be performed. It was a bribe to the Irish bishops to hold Ireland—in co-operation with the British police and soldiery—a province of England. The millions of dollars, expended by the English government on Maynooth college, have been well and fully repaid. Every student entering that college had first, before he could be ordained priest, to take this oath:

THE MAYNOOTH OATH,

IN WHICH EVERY PRIEST SWEARS TO DISCLOSE ALL TREASONS AGAINST THE ENGLISH SOVEREIGN.

I, A. B., do hereby declare that I profess the Roman Catholic religion. I, A. B., do sincerely promise and swear that I will be faithful, and bear true allegiance to his Majesty King George the Third, "and him will I defend to the

utmost of my power AGAINST ALL CONSPIRACIES
and attempts whatsoever that shall be made against his
person, crown, or dignity; and I will do my utmost
endeavor to disclose and make known to His Majesty, his
heirs and successors, ALL TREASONS and traitorous conspiracies which may be formed against him or them; and
I do faithfully promise to maintain, support and defend, to
the utmost of my power, the successor of the crown;
which succession, by an act entitled an act for the further
limitation of the crown, and the better securing the rights
and liberties of the subject, is and stands limited to the
Prince Sophia, Electress and Duchess Dowager of Hanover
and the heirs of her body, being Protestants: hereby utterly
renouncing and abjuring obedience or pretending a right to
the crown of these realms; and I do swear that I reject
and detest as an unchristian and impious position, that it is
lawful to murder or destroy any person or persons whatsoever, for or under pretense of their being heretics or infidels, and also that unchristian and impious principle that
faith is not to be kept with heretics or infidels; and I further declare that it is not an article of my faith, and that I
do renounce, reject and abjure the opinion that princes,
excommunicated by the pope and council or by any authority of the see of Rome, or by any authority whatsoever,
may be deposed and murdered by their subjects, or by any
person whatsoever; and I do promise that I will not hold,
maintain or abet any such opinion or any other opinion
contrary to what is expressed in this declaration; and I do
declare that I do not believe that the pope of Rome, or any
other foreign prince, prelate, state or potentate hath or
ought to have any temporal or civil jurisdiction, power,
superiority, or pre-eminence, directly or indirectly, within
this realm; and I do solemnly, in the presence of God,
profess, testify and declare that I do make this declaration,
and every part thereof, in the plain and ordinary sense of
the words of this oath, without any evasion, equivocation
or mental reservation whatever, and without any dispensa-
tion already granted by the pope, or any authority of the

see of Rome, or any person whatever, and without thinking that I am or can be acquitted before God or man, or
absolved of this declaration, or any part thereof, although
the pope or any other person or authority whatsoever
shall dispense with or annul the same or declare that it is
null or void, so help me God."

England paid $150,000 a year to the Irish hierarchy—
the trustees of Maynooth—on condition that the ecclesiastics educated there would act as spies and informers for
England afterwards. This is the amount of the affair.
Scores of noble young Irishmen—to their immortal honor
be it said—crossed the seas, and paid for their education
in France, in Spain, or in some other country, rather than
subscribe to this humiliating oath. This oath was continued
down to the accession of the present monarch, Queen Vic-
toria, and far into her reign.

THE DESTRUCTION OF IRELAND'S PARLIAMENT.

The next maneuvre of the British government was to
rob Ireland of her parliament; and in the accomplishment
of this design, English statesmen sought and received the
aid of the Irish hierarchy. Lord Castlereagh—in whose
hands the Catholic bishops were but as so many children—
was the prime wirepuller in this plot. Says the Nun of
Kenmare (History of Ireland, p. 220):

SERVICE RENDERED BY THE IRISH BISHOPS TO ENGLAND, IN HELP-
ING TO CARRY THE "ACT OF UNION."

"It is to be regretted that the Catholic bishops, who
worked for the Union, did not see some of the private correspondence in which they were mentioned, and did not
hear some of the private conversations which have been
recorded and sent down to posterity. Sir J. Hippsley, who
was specially employed to cajole the Catholics, wrote to
Lord Castlereagh:

"The Speaker told me, some time before, that Mr. Pitt

had much approved the suggestions I had offered, with
respect to the distinction and checks on the monastic
clergy. Your lordship will permit me to quote a vulgar
Italian proverb, which is this: 'One must be aware of a
bull before, of an ass at his heels, and of a friar on all
sides.' Seven years' experience on Catholic grounds con-
vinced me that this adage was well imagined."

"On the 5th of June, 1799, the Earl of Altamont wrote
from Westport House: 'The priests have all appeared to
sign; and though I am not proud of many of them as asso-
ciates, I will take their signatures to prevent a possibility of
a counter declaration.'"

"On the 3d of June, 1799, Lord Castlereagh wrote to
the Duke of Portland that the rebellion was managed by
'the inferior priests.' There were certainly some of the
Catholic clergy who united with the rebels, in self-defense;
but a careful examination of the correspondence of the
times will show at once that they were few in number, and
that the government relied much on the co-operation of
the priests, even at the very time that many of them were
being treated with inhuman cruelty. On the 20th of July,
1799, Lord Cornwallis wrote, to the Duke of Portland, that
the clergy of the church, particularly the superior, coun-
tenanced the measure; and that the linen-merchants of
the north were much too busy with their trade to think
much on the subject."

Lord Castlereagh deemed Catholic support "absolutely
necessary" to the success of his infamous project. He so
declared himself. Quoting from some of his private letters, Sister Clare (p. 244) writes:

CASTLEREAGH WORKING FOR CATHOLIC INFLUENCE TO CARRY THE
UNION.

"Lord Castlereagh wrote a 'most private' letter to the
Right Honorable William Pitt, on the 1st of January, 1801,
in which he puts the whole state of the case into the plain-
est possible language, in which he showed how absolutely

necessary the assistance of the Catholic body was in order
to carry the union; and how he had been ordered to draw
the Catholics on. The object was gained; and, if there
was not another document in existence, besides this letter,
to show how shamefully the Catholics were duped, it would
be more than sufficient. At last, with considerable difficulty, the upper class of Catholics, (i. e., the bishops, priests
and aristocracy) were made to understand how they had
been treated. It might have been supposed that they had
learned a life-long lesson; but there are persons on whom
experience is wasted."

ENGLAND'S ATTEMPT TO ENSLAVE THE IRISH CHURCH.

THE IRISH HIERARCHY CONSENT THAT THE ENGLISH GOVERNMENT SHALL PENSION THE PRIESTS AND HAVE THE RIGHT TO VETO CANDIDATES FOR BISHOPS.

At first England made war upon Ireland's nationality.
Then England tore away from Ireland her parliament; and
now England comes forward, and with unblushing audacity
asks the Catholic bishops of Ireland to recognize the English king as the virtual head of the Catholic church in Ireland; and, (will the astounding revelation be believed?) the
four archbishops of Ireland, with six other bishops, trustees
of Maynooth, accepted the proposition! This they did
after due deliberation in convention. Not only did they
concede this, but they consented furthermore that the
priests of Ireland should be lowered to the level of pen-
sioned officials of the British government. McGee tells of
the transaction as follows, in his book entitled "Attempts
to Establish the Protestant Reformation in Ireland," p. 284:

"On the 17th, 18th and 19th of January, 1789, the
bishops, who were Maynooth trustees, sat at Dublin, 'to
deliberate on a proposal from government for an independent provision (i. e. a pension) for the Roman Catholic
clergy of Ireland, under certain regulations not incompat-

ible with their doctrine, discipline or just influence.' A
minute of this meeting, signed by the four archbishops and
the bishops of Meath, Cork, Kildare, Elphin, Ferns, and
Ardagh, was approved and submitted to the ministers. The
'certain regulations' were, in a word, to control the appointment of bishops, to give government a veto on bishops
elect. The ten prelates just mentioned agreed to lay before
government the names of the nominees; they undertaking
to 'transmit the name of said candidate, if no objection
be made against him, for appointment to the holy see,'
within a month of receiving it. Further the prelates agreed
'If government have any próper objection against such
candidates, the president of the election will be informed
thereof within one month after the presentation, who in
that case, will convene the electors to the election of another candidate.' By this undertaking, Primate O'Reilly
and the hierarchy, in 1799, granted to the State what
[another] primate O'Reilly and the hierarchy, in 1666, suffered exile and death rather than concede. Fortunately for
the Irish church, the state neglected to conclude the compact at that time."

"And here let us glance at the temporal evils inflicted on
the Irish people through this outrage done to Ireland's
nationality. But the injury done to the church itself was
no less great. Says the Nun of Kenmare, referring to the
EVIL EFFECTS OF IRELAND'S SUBJECTION TO ENGLISH DOMINATION;

"One fearful evil followed from this Anglo-Norman invasion. The Irish clergy had hitherto been distinguished for
the high tone of their moral conduct; the English clergy
unhappily were not so rich in this virtue; and their evil
communication had a most injurious effect upon the nation
whom it was supposed they should be so eminently capable
of benefiting."

It will be seen now that neither Ireland nor true religion gained anything by the blow given to Ireland's nationality.

THE CHURCH'S LOSS.

In 1836, Bishop England estimated the Catholic population of this country at 1,200,000. The total population of the United States then was fifteen millions. The number of persons lost to the church in fifty years, preceding 1836, was, says Bishop England, 3,750,000.

"If I say," adds Dr. England, "upon the foregoing data, that we ought, if there were no loss, to have 5,000,000 of Catholics and that we have less than one million and a quarter, there must be a loss of three millions and three-quarters, at least; and the persons so lost are found among the various sects to the amount of thrice the number of the Catholic population of the whole country."—[Works of Bishop England, vol. 3, page 126–127.]

Bishop England did not attempt to estimate the loss of the hundred and fifty years preceding 1836.

The Catholic population of the United States to-day is some ten millions. But the number of persons who ought to be Catholics by right of descent from settlers in this country, from the beginning, and who to-day are to be found among the sects or in the ranks of Nothingarianism, is estimated at eighteen millions.—[See statistics and proofs in Irish World of July 25, 1874.]

WE ARE ALWAYS GUARDED.

CHARACTER OF THE ANGLO-CATHOLIC ARISTOCRACY—EVEN THE BEST OF THEM A MISERABLE SET.

But the Catholic Englishman (we speak of the rule) is the cunning creature who, at Rome, always gives a bad name to Ireland's patriots, and who, whilst using the Irish for his own purposes, despises the Irish in the depth of his heart. We have no pleasure in saying this; but this is the fact; and we cannot deny it. Listen to Father Burke. In his "sermons and lectures," p. 219, Father Burke, speak-

ing of Englishmen—even English Catholics, his own per-
sonal friends—says:

"My friends, I know the English people well. Some of
the best friends that I have in the world are in England.
They have a great many fine qualities: but there is a secret
passive contempt for Ireland and for Irishmen."

Hear what the Sister of Clare says of the English Catholics. The English Catholic aristocracy, even at the time
they needed the political aid of the Irish most, scorned to
associate with them! Such was their utter contempt for
the mere Irish. Sister Clare (Life of O'Connell, p. 424)
says:

"We have already said something of the political opin-
ions of English Catholics. They made then the fatal mis-
take of disassociating themselves from their Irish brethren.
We have seen how some of them were even willing to
forego the name of Catholic, and their self-respect along
with it, for the miserable imaginary advantage of a higher
social respectability. It is a matter of history, that the
great majority—that, in fact, an overwhelming majority of
English Catholics apostatized from their religion, to preserve their worldly goods. A noble few remained faithful;
but the leaven of worldliness was at work even amongst
these few; and they readily listened to any specious plea
which would tend to lessen that isolation from their Protestant fellow-countrymen, which they felt to be, and which
was, a social bar sinister."

HOSTILITY OF ENGLISH CATHOLICS TO IRISH.

In 1829, O'Connell won Catholic Emancipation. It was
the English Catholic aristocracy, and not the Irish people,
who gained anything by the measure. Yet when O'Connell
began his repeal movement, the English Catholics became
his most virulent enemies. In a letter written by Daniel
O'Connell (Nov. 9, 1873,) to Archbishop MacHale, he says:

"Dr. England was with me yesterday; he gave me some
strong evidence of hostility of the English Catholics to

those of Ireland. He has promised to give it to me in
writing; and I will send your grace a copy."

The English Catholic is to-day as he has ever been. Such
is the testimony of Bishop England. Such was O'Connell's.
Such is the experience of every Irishman. Niall the Grand
is not an exception. ·

And now, let me say, with wealth and honors came in-
trigues and conspiracies, and plottings for place among
churchmen and princes, and general corruption in church
and state. A king would thrust a creature of his own into
the papal chair, and maintain him by force of arms. Some-
times Christendom would be scandalized at the spectacle of
three anti-popes. Spain would recognize one, France another, and Germany a third. All these anti-popes would
be fulminating bulls and excommunications against one
another. The minor priests, too, did as they liked. What
was the result of all this? What does church history tell?
Slavery among the people; ignorance among the clergy;
strifes among the bishops as to who should be first; rapacity and immorality amongst all classes; continual wars
among rulers, and heresies and schisms in the Universal
church. These were the fruits of ecclesiastical wealth and
honors! Greece fell away from the church. With Greece
may be counted that immense country, Russia, which now
numbers sixty millions of people. The churches of Asia
Minor, of Egypt, and other parts of Africa, as well as of
other countries, had long since rotted and perished. Then
in the sixteenth century followed Germany; then Sweden;
then Norway; then England; then Scotland, with portions
of France and Switzerland. All these countries apostatized because the priesthood were corrupt and worldly.

His Eminence, Cardinal Cullen, in his time, in his lenten
pastorals, denounced "sedition, revolution, Fenianism and
Ribbonism," and orders that all persons, connected in any
way with those who hold meetings, balls, etc., in support
of such principles, shall be deemed by their spiritual direc-
tors thereby guilty of sin. This was a widespread and an

astounding declaration against all of us who are laboring
for a revolution—that is, a change in the political and social
condition of four or five millions of Irishmen and women
in Ireland. "Sedition!" If the word mean anything at
all, it is the expression of people's dissatisfaction with something that annoys, impedes, troubles, injures them. Lord
Castlereagh, of glorious and pious memory, brought into
the English parliament several acts to repress free speech,
one of which was a bill to repress and punish sedition; and
"sedition" was defined by this bill to be "the uttering
and publishing of words tending to bring the government
and laws of the country into hatred and contempt." Well,
there are the laws of England, operating in Ireland for 700
years past; and you who speak in hatred and contempt of
these laws must have been committing sin against God all
the time: and those Cardinals tell you there is for you no
sacramental forgiveness, unless you repent of the sin, and
leave off speaking or writing in hatred of the laws which
England has forced upon Ireland at the point of the bayonet. Revolution was also denounced by His Eminence as
sinful. Now, revolution means change. For instance: the
change or revolution which, over one hundred years ago,
converted the thirteen dependent colonies of England in
North America into a glorious republic, the "United States
of America," into which ten or twelve millions of His
Eminence's countrymen have expatriated themselves, escap-
ing from Ireland and the horrors of its English governors
as best they could, and finding, as a result of that change,
homes, wages, education, religious and political liberty, free
lands and free schools, to ask for which at home was deemed
rank sedition, a punishable crime; the same now being in
the eyes of His Eminence, Cardinal Cabe, a punishable sin.
Yet, there is no place on the habitable globe where the
religion of His Eminence is more respected, better observed
and more substantially supported than in this glorious
republic.

His Eminence condemned "secret societies" as tending
to generate immorality, sensuality, etc. It is a matter to

create surprise that there are some secret societies in the
world which have received the blessings of the Catholic
Church, through the precious hands of the holy father himself. For instance, King Alfonso was called to the throne
of Spain, a few years ago, by a thoroughly 'secret society'
composed of grandees, generals, priests, lawyers, and others of the Spanish aristocracy; and the head of that secret
society, as soon as they thought the "pear ripe" for proclaiming him king, obtained the prompt blessing of the
holy father. Don Carlos VII., of Spain, is head, also, of
another secret society, in which many of the nobility and
Catholic clergy of Europe are enrolled and are contributors,
the object of which is to place Don Carlos, by force of arms,
even to the point of the bayonet, on the throne of Spain,
as ruler over an unwilling people, who prefer to rule themselves and make their own laws without the assistance of
such a red-handed legislator. His holiness, on April 12,
1874, blessed the wife of Don Carlos, on her safe delivery
of a daughter, addressing and congratulating her as "your
Majesty"—as Queen of Spain. There was another secret
society established in France in the year 1874, whose object
it was to bring over the Count de Chambord to rule the
French people on the good old plans that prevailed under
the "white flag" of his Bourbon ancestors; which plans,
if restored, would compel all the small landed-proprietors
of France, of whom there are six millions, to resign their
lands to the descendants of the old nobility of France, the
"Emigres" of '89-'93, and to become again their tenants
and serfs, as in the good old times of the Louises. The
Catholic Bishop of Orleans and the Catholic Archbishop
of Paris commanded all their cures to call from their pulpits upon their various congregations, on the holy Sabbath,
to pray to God for the restoration of the Bourbon King.
That was another "secret society" which the church did
not condemn. All this appears incompatible with Cardinal
McCabe's dicta. Is there liberty in the church for kings,
lords and bishops to conspire secretly to effect their purposes; and is this liberty denied and punished by exclusion

from religious sacraments, in the common people, who toil
to produce the wealth which the others may appropriate
by laws of their own making? Can this be regarded as
the equity of religion?

The Fenians were condemned by their Eminences Cullen
and McCabe, in their pastorals. Now the ten, who denounce the "IRISH WORLD" in Cincinnati, are of the same
type.

Why? The Fenians conceived that a change was
required in the laws—in their making and their administer-
ing in Ireland. A conception growing from centuries of
misrule—centuries of landlord oppression—growing from
the destruction of two hundred and forty thousand peasant
dwellings, the quenching of two hundred and forty thous-
and hearth-fires in Ireland, within the last twenty years,
and the scattering of millions of men, women and children
of Ireland over all parts of the globe, by forcible evictions
from their homesteads, even by the aid of the police and
army. The Fenians conspired to overthrow the heartless
men, who compassed and effected these national outrages.
They did some of the work which they contemplated.
They broke down forever religious ascendancy in Ireland.
The Irish Church establishment is gone, never to return;
and it was abolished by the Fenians, and by the Fenians
alone. An incision has been made in the land monopoly,
which will be widened, day by day, hereafter. Instead of
gratitude for this, the Fenians have curses loud and deep;
for did not Cardinal Cullen excommunicate them from his
church; and has not Bishop Moriarity judged them—yes,
judged them—and condemned them to hell, regretting that
hell was not hot enough nor eternity long enough to inflict
sufficient punishment!

The whole career of Cardinal Cullen as Archbishop and
Cardinal, in Ireland, has been singularly marked by opposition to every effort and aspiration of the Irish people to
relieve themselves from the galling tyranny; and now Cardinal McCabe, his blood relation, does the same service.
Oh! "Irish!"

OATH OF THE EMANCIPATED CATHOLIC OFFICE-SEEKER.

"I, A. B., do sincerely promise and swear that I will be faithful and bear true allegiance to His Majesty King George the Fourth, and will defend him to the utmost of my power against all conspiracies and attempts whatever which shall be made against his person, crown or dignity; and I will do my utmost endeavor to disclose and make known to His Majesty, his heirs and successors, all treasons and traitorous conspiracies which may be formed against him or them; and I do faithfully promise to maintain, support and defend, to the utmost of my power, the succession of the crown, which succession, by an act entitled 'An act for the further limitation of the Crown, and better securing the rights and liberties of the subject,' is and stands limited to the Princess Sophia, Electress of Hanover, and the heirs of her body, being Protestants, hereby utterly renouncing and abjuring any obedience or allegiance unto any other person claiming or pretending a right to the crown of these realms; and I do further declare that it is not an article of my faith, and that I do renounce, reject and abjure the opinion that princes excommunicated or deprived by the pope, or any other authority of the see of Rome, may be deposed or murdered by their subjects or by any person whatsoever; and I do declare that I do not believe that the pope of Rome or any other foreign prince, prelate, person, state or potentate hath or ought to have any temporal or civil jurisdiction, power, superiority, pre-eminence, directly or indirectly, within this realm. I do swear that I will defend, to the utmost of my power, the settlement of property, within this realm, as established by the laws; and I do hereby disclaim, disavow, and solemnly abjure any intention to subvert the present church establishment as settled by law within this realm; and I do solemnly swear that I never will exercise any privilege to which I am or may become entitled, to disturb or weaken the Protestant religion or Protestant government in this kingdom: and I do solemnly, in the presence of God profess, testify and declare that I do make this declaration, and every part thereof, in the plain and ordinary sense of words of this oath, without any evasion, equivocation, or mental reservation whatsoever."

> The heart of Erin everywhere to-day
>   Throbs with the magic of a mighty love ;
> "God bless his life and death," the millions pray,
>   "And crown him with celestial light above !"

> Aye, take him to your hearts, ye exiled band;
>   For who more worthy of the love of Gael
> Than he whose name is blest in every land—
>   True patriot-priest, immortal JOHN McHALE !

Sursum Corda, (Be not disheartened).

IRELAND'S BONDAGE.

THE YOKE MADE TIGHTER BY POLITICO-RELIGIOUS AGENCIES.

Can Ireland gain her independence so long as the influence of the clergy is on the side of the English? It is apparent to all liberal-minded men that O'Connell's failure was partly if not entirely caused by the influence of the clergy. That this influence has had its headquarters at Rome is evident from the testimony of the late Mr. Greville, who was for over forty years clerk of the English Privy Council. He has stated in his published memoirs that, during all his time, there never was a Catholic bishop appointed by the pope, in Ireland, with only one exception, who had not previously been approved and indicated to his holiness by the English agent in Rome—and the single exception, in forty years, was MacHale. Reader, if you are an Irishman, a little reflection on the following sad story of the great Fenian movement will be advantageous to you; therefore, save this hurriedly-written sketch of the history of our country. Are not the men such as Bishop Gilmore more dangerous to religion and morals than laymen? The story of the failure of the Fenians is introduced, here, with all due respect for the men who upheld that godlike spirit of resistance to British rule in Ireland.

HOW SHALL WE FREE IRELAND?

This is a question that for many a long age has occupied the minds of the deepest thinkers of the Irish race. O'Connell, at one period of his life, had the freedom of Ireland in the palm of his hands. When he stood on Tara Hill, on the 15th of August, 1843, with a million men around him,

with the English Chartists, the French Republicans and the
whole American nation at his back, he might then have
declared the independence of Ireland, and there was no
force in England (as Peel admitted,) to restrain him. But,
ambitious to establish a new force in political agitations, he
rudely rejected the co-operation of the English Chartists;
politely declined all aid from the French Republicans,
though tendered to him by Ledru Rollin, their chief; to the
Southern Americans he flung back their money with scorn
because it came from slaveholders ; and he denounced the
sons and friends of the '98 men as miscreants. When Peel
saw that O'Connell had thus cast away with contempt all
promises of physical aid, he seized upon him, clapped him
into prison, broke the spell which his voice and name had
spread over the Irish race, and which he (O'Connell) never
after re-established. From that day our cause and hopes
declined ; and a whole generation has grown up in despair,
in ignorance of their rights, and in fear almost of asserting
any claim at all to national rights. Opposed to this general
decline appeared, in the dark days of utter despair,

THE FENIANS.

Yes, they came to the front equipped only with resolve,
with a remarkable daring, but defective organization. Even
though badly led, they frightened England into some nom-
inal concessions which are useful only in making us understand what could be won from her (England), if the Fenians had been able to concentrate their scattered forces in
the Southern or Western mountains ; and if they had not
been cursed from almost every Catholic altar, and set to
the English enemy by many (too many) Catholic clergymen.
It puzzles an Irishman to account for the hostility of the
Roman Catholic bishops (with one or two exceptions) to
our Irish National Independence. I have read, and never
shall forget, the able review which appeared in the mem-
orable IRISH WORLD of May 15th, where you say :

"If you are a priest, and are placed over an Irish congregation, and if you see any Fenians perverting the people

and saying that we, the Irish race in America, ought to do
something for Ireland, fiercely denounce those bad men.
Tell the people that the Irish ought to be loyal to England,
even in persecutions. Tell them the Irish are persecuted
in this world because they are good Christians. Tell them
that those persecutions have proved wonderfully beneficial
—that the expulsion of the mere Irish from their own
homes, with their dispersion abroad, has brought the Mar-
quis of Bute, the Earl of Ripon, and a score of gentlemen
and superannuated countesses to the faith, (but of the millions lost to the faith, the descendants of the mere Irish in
England and America, you need not tell). Repeat these
things again and again. Tell the people that they must not
be too much troubled about the temporal interests of Ireland—that patriotism is a deceptive sentiment—that this
world anyhow, with all its vanity, will pass away ; and that
therefore, as good Christians, they ought not to set their
hearts upon it. This is the style of some priests and
bishops."

AGAINST IRISH FREEDOM.

You have described most truly, sir, in the above passage,
the proceedings and ecclesiastical policy of certain Catholic
bishops and priests in America. To this accurate guage, I
would, with your permission, supplement a few plain facts
from the British government side of the question. To the
really zealous Nationalists, who desire to get poor old Ireland re-established a nation among the nations, no impedi-
ment is so distressing, so unaccountable, so hard to be
dealt with as the opposition, which comes from the Roman
Catholic hierarchy and many of the priesthood, to every
thorough, every substantial effort to emancipate our dear
country. Why this unnatural hatred of our freedom exists
I cannot pretend to answer ; but, that it does exist and is
actively propagated, I am in a condition to prove. Having
spent a winter in Rome lately, I have learned considerable
of English manipulations—what the French call " en
plusier's manieres "—something concerning their round-
about methods of manufacturing chains in Rome to man-

acle the Irish in Ireland. To explain how this is done, to
the understanding of the common people—that is the toil-
ing classes—I must ask liberal space in your precious col-
umns. It had been the unconcealed desire of the govern-
ing oligarchy of England—the landlords—for many years
past, to get some control, little or much, in the appointment
of the Catholic bishops of Ireland. In O'Connell's lifetime,
during his struggle for

CATHOLIC EMANCIPATION,

the proposal was made to him that if he would consent to
give the English government this desired control, it would
pave an easy way to his Catholic emancipation. That great
measure was kept back for years, because he and the bulk
of the Irish people refused to the English government this
veto privilege, which would, if granted, compel all candidates for bishops' mitres in Ireland to have their names
submitted to the British monarch, and be approved by that
monarch, before their acceptance and consecration by the
pope in Rome. A second wing of security, sought to be
added to the emancipation act, was a state payment of
annual salaries to the Irish Catholic clergy ; and a third, the
abolition of the voting powers of the forty-shilling free-
holders. The first two O'Connell rejected ; the last he
agreed to, which disfranchised at least five hundred thousand voters in Ireland ; for consenting to which he was
afterwards sorry enough. O'Connell emancipated the
Catholics of Ireland, England and Scotland, and the Dis-
senters also ; for which some of the said English are not
over grateful. Emancipation would have been still refused
but for fear of an Irish insurrection. This is admitted in
Sir Robert Peel's Memoirs, and by the Duke of Wellington
in his speech introducing the measure in the House of
Lords.

THE FENIAN MEN.

Now came a new generation of Fenian men, who saw
nothing more in Catholic Emancipation than a road opened
to enable Mr. —— and Mr. —— 'and Mr. —— to

enter parliament, make themselves heard there, get to be
solicitors-general, attorneys-general, governors of colonies;
then assistant barristers, stipendiary magistrates; then
judges on the bench, and other offices of profit and honor,
whereby they may dress in purple and fine linen, and sit in
judgment, enabling the Irish landlords to dispossess the
people of their lands according to law, while the millions of
Catholics may go to the emigrant ship, to Hong Kong, or to
the d——l! Now comes the Fenian agitation—an agitation
somewhat different in its objects from the former. What
could England do with that? It was, in the eyes of foreign
powers, an ugly crack in the British breastplate, this Fenian
cry for the land and for an Irish republic!—a cry which
O'Connell in his philosophy never dreamed of. Could she
get Rome to do anything to stop it. Let us trace her tortuous policy in that city.

FATHER CULLEN.

About fifty-seven years ago, there came to Rome from
Ireland a student for the priesthood, a son not of the peer-
age but of the peasantry of Kildare, who has subsequently
become a "personage" in the world. He entered the
Irish College in Rome; and by his studious, careful and
conservative habits, rose step by step to be superior of the
college, whose average number of students ranged at about
fifty; whose course of education was pretty strictly con-
fined to theology, and the histories, and the arguments
springing therefrom. The position of superior of this Irish
college the priest maintained for twenty years, in strict
seclusion, which brought him the acquaintance of all the
high dignitaries connected with the Sacred College of Cardinals. This was Father Cullen, the Superior of the Irish
College at Rome. I would next make the reader acquainted with

CARDINAL ANTONELLI,

who has filled the post of Secretary to the College of Cardinals—that is, Secretary of State to the Roman Catholic
church throughout the world—for at least thirty years past,

through whom all the correspondence of all the ecclesiastics and crowned heads throughout the world passes to the Pope, is registered, noted, brought under consideration of the Sacred Council, and replied to. Now, this great personage, though filling the highest office in the Catholic Church next to the Holy Father, is not a priest in orders, and never was. But he is a very able linguist, is master of a score of languages, is able to do with little sleep and little food, can answer more letters, and does answer more letters, in a day than do all the British Ministers in the same space of time. This extraordinary man was in youth a poor boy from the mountains, who got into one of the colleges as a servant, and swallowed all sorts of knowledge with unusual gusto. His sheer ability of mind and body brought him under the notice of the predecessor of Pius IX., who placed him in the correspondence department of the Holy See, in which office he was continued by the present Pope; and without passing through the graditory steps of the eglise, was endowed with the commanding title of Cardinal. The Cardinal-Secretary is the dispenser of dignities, appointments, places and power throughout the whole church. All, who want favors from the Holy See, from the crowned head ruler of a nation, down to the humble cure or priest of a parish, present their suit to the Cardinal. It is the custom, of those who seek favors at his hand, to propitiate him with some present. The very rich give jeweled snuff boxes or gems of vast value; the poorer suitors bring coined gold to his shrine. His palace is, next to the Vatican, the richest magazine of gems, jewels and works of art of great value in Rome. His Eminence is engaged daily in arranging and classifying his wondrous store, which (it is said by clergymen) would purchase a principality. Of course, such a man is a strict conservator of "order," hates changes, and is, indeed, the chief man that arrested the reforming hand of Pius IX., in 1846, when His Holiness had joined the father of King Victor Emanuel in his attempt to drive the Austrians from Italian soil. In his mind, the powers that be are the powers to obey, pro-

vided those powers have in their veins any of the pure
blood of kings.

PETRE, THE ENGLISH AGENT.

I would now introduce another important character in
this painful story. There were in Rome twenty years ago,
as there are at present, certain political agents of the British Government—not open, recognized agents, mind you,
but "tourists," "artists," of the Sir Patrick O'Plenipo
class, among whom was a young Englishman, the Hon.
Mr. Petre, son of Lord Petre, an English Catholic gentleman who lived much in Rome; for he was an ardent
admirer and student of art. He was very intimate with
Cardinal Antonelli and the other chief princes. To the
Cardinal, the troubles of the English Government with the
Irish revolutionary characters were made known. It was
easily made manifest, to His Eminence, that revolutionary
aspirations in Ireland would tend to ignite latent members
of a similar nature in England, and elsewhere in Europe,
and that, in the interests of "society" and "order," his
aid was evoked to suppress, by the crushing power of the
church, all such dangerous manifestations. The Irish bishops—aye, they were the springs of Irish sentiment, the
channels, in fact, which must guide Irish thought in its flow
—these were the keys to the heart of the Irish nation; and
in order to preserve the peace of Europe, they were to be
influenced, even coerced, to suppress all "dangerous societies" of whatsoever name or object in Ireland.

BRITISH FRIENDSHIP IN RETURN.

In return for His Eminence's interference, in the manner
suggested, the Queen of England would become the active
friend of the temporal power, and would discountenance
and discourage, through her peers and commoners, and
denounce, through all her magazines and newspapers, the
Garibaldis and Mazzinis of Italian revolution. Nothing
could be more reasonable and proper than all this to the
minds of the Cardinal and his eminent brethren of the

Sacred College, the majority of whom are always of Italian birth, and know about as much of Irish history as they do of one of the South American republics. So the Irish priesthood were to be muzzled; the Lavelles, the McQuaids, the Andersons, the Vaughans and the MacHales were to be put under the ban, and all their seditious mouths to be closed. Although they are witnesses—aye, eye-witnesses of the destruction of thousands of Irish dwellings, the eviction from their lands of hundreds of thousands of industrious Roman Catholic people, they are forbidden to open their mouths in complaint against landlords who promote or the government which permits these calamitous outrages.

FATHER CULLEN RAISED TO POWER.

A most fortunate opportunity arrived to put this British policy into active operation. Dr. Curtis, primate of Armagh, died, a successor was duly and legally named by a convocation of the clergy of the diocese. Three names were voted for by the convention, according to immemorial usage, and sent on to Rome with their respective characters appended to each, viz: Dignus (worthy, Dignoir (worthier), Dignissimus (most worthy), from which three His Holiness was, according to custom, to select one to fill the chair of Primate of Ireland. But instead of this, His Holiness, at the promptings and advice of somebody in Rome, passed over and ignored the three clergymen sent to him by the Irish Diocese Convention, and took a priest of the Irish College in Rome from his books and his pupils and his solitude in St. Agatha's, and appointed him

ARCHBISHOP AND PRIMATE,

and sent him to rule over the heads of all the clergy of Ireland. This gentleman was Dr. Paul Cullen, the celebrated public enemy of the Fenians and the private friend of the British Empire. This appointment suited the British government completely. The new Irish Primate was the second self of Cardinal Antonelli. The "Church" was to get privileges, in all the British colonies where the Catholic bishops and priests are stipendiaries of the British Government. The Bishops get from £500 to £700 a year; the priests from £150 to £200 a year salaries, throughout the principal colonies of Her Majesty's empire. There are many other privileges also, which the "church" (that is the bishops) obtained as a consideration for yielding up Ireland in chains to her relentless oppressor.

CONDEMNS FRENCH ASSISTANCE.

His first services to his new masters were performed by the new primate in the year 1859; and this is the manner and method of them. After the failure of the Young Irelanders' attempt at insurrection, in 1848, many of the leaders were driven out of Ireland. Some were transported to the far off colonies; some took refuge in New York, others in Paris, and some returned to their homes in obscurity, in the south of Ireland. Although the attempt at a rising was at the time suppressed, the aspiration for national independence was not stamped out. The signs most hopeful of its ultimate success are found in the cool business-like manner in which the baffled, defeated Irish patriots go again to their work, as if nothing ill had happened to them in previous attempts! Well, an organization was effected between the men in Ireland and their friends in Paris and America, to make another attempt. The mode of the next move had not yet gotten shape. It was understood among the leaders, that the late Emperor of the French, Louis Napoleon, would favor the designs of the Irish "Phœnix men"—this being the appellation of the Irish patriots then. Napoleon had some negotiations on foot with England, touching the admission of French manufactures and French wines into England at a reduced duty, and the better to help his negotiations, he built those famous sea-monsters in Cherbourg, which created consternation in England. But when he invited John Mitchell from America to Paris, this was the climax. All England was in a panic. The funds fell in price, when it was known that Mitchell had actually come to Paris. It was then that

Archbishop Cullen was wanted by the British Government, and speedily he came to their aid. In the nick of time he issued his celebrated "Pastoral" to the priests and people of Ireland, warning them against "French infidels," French "anarchists," and all that, saying to his flock, EX CATHEDRA, that "he would rather see the Irish people suffer another seven years' famine than accept aid or political association from the infidel French!" and this, mind you, at the very time that Cardinal Antonelli had twenty thousand French soldiers in Rome and its suburbs, supporting the kingly power of the Pope! The French Emperor was stunned by the appearance of this remarkable pastoral, and feeling that to help the Irish in an insurrection against England, with the Catholic clergy against it, would be disastrous to the design, he got chilled over the enterprise. In addition to his motives for holding back, Her Majesty, the Queen of England, journeyed over to France to meet the Emperor, and did meet him, and kiss him too! The kiss of a queen has, we know, a wondrous power. Even Julius Cæsar, stern though he was known to be, was melted by the kiss of Cleopatra. Our queen, it is true, is not a Cleopatra; yet her kiss, together with the Archbishop's pastoral and the concessions to the Emperor of his international demands killed, for the time, in its embryonic state, the Phœnix insurrection. The pastorals of the Archbishops, at that time, had much greater weight and influence with the Irish than they have had latterly.

THE MACMANUS FUNERAL.

I will now advance in my mournful story. Terrence Bellew MacManus died in San Francisco sometime in the year 1861—died in care of the Sisters of Mercy, in their hospital, having previously received the last sacrament of his church. The Irish of that city gave him a splendid funeral, laid him in the Catholic cemetery of Lone Mountain. A meeting was subsequently held in San Francisco, to erect a monument over his remains, at which meeting it was proposed, and, after some discussion, resolved to raise the body and send it to Ireland for interment. It was to be taken to New York, where the Irish were to co-operate in taking charge of the body, and thence to Cork, where, on landing, the Cork men were to organize a slow funeral procession by the high road from Cork to Dublin, to pause at intervals in the journey, and have orations pronounced over the dead rebel. That was the programme; and it was pretty nearly carried out. These honors were offered to MacManus because, though no general, he bravely joined Smith O'Brien and the others in facing British power in the field; and here it must be noted that Smith O'Brien was totally unfitted, by nature or experience, to lead an armed insurrection against England, as was very quickly perceived by the common people in the South of Ireland, who declined to fight when they heard him proclaim that the army of insurrection was to purchase their rations with hard cash. But he was honored, nevertheless, and so were MacManus and Meagher, because they had risked life and were tried and condemned to death in Clonmel, to be there hanged, drawn and quartered for their attempt to free Ireland.

THE IRISH RACE IN AMERICA

and in Ireland had unanimously decreed funeral honors to the remains of MacManus. The body was received in the cathedrals by bishops, and a solemn mass for the dead was offered for the repose of the soul of him who risked life, liberty and lost trade and position for Ireland. When the body arrived on Irish earth, it was taken to the Catholic chapel in Queenstown, where it was received by Doctor Keene, at the chapel door, and there again a solemn sacrifice of Holy mass for the dead was offered over the body. At every station between Cork and Dublin crowds of people appeared, anxious to take the body out of the railway carriages and carry it on their shoulders, according to the original programme, which, I must say, they ought to have been permitted to do. Arrived in Dublin, thousands and tens of thousands were ready to take part in the great

national funeral: but first, application was made to Archbishop Cullen, (who at this time had been translated from
Armagh to Dublin,) to offer a solemn mass for the dead
over the body, at his cathedral, Marlborough street. To
this very natural request, the Archbishop replied that he
required twenty-four hour's consideration, before he could
give an answer. "Twenty-four hours' consideration" to
study whether an Irish Catholic child of the church, who
died in its bosom in a foreign land, should obtain through
the united prayers of his ten thousand friends, the benefits
of their united prayers at holy mass, for the repose of his
soul. The American conductors of the funeral soon saw
through the mind of the Archbishop, and rightly read the
excuse of the pro-English ecclesiastic, which was that " the
funeral bore a political aspect, and he did not desire that he
and the church should be mixed up with it," whereupon

FATHER LAVELLE

issued his famous address, beginning: " Ireland! Ireland!
has it come to this?" etc. The body of MacManus was
taken to its resting place in Glasnevin; the layman from
San Francisco, in charge of it, a Colonel Smith, uttered a
discourse over it; and Father Lavelle made the last prayer
over the body as it was lowered down, which, it is hoped,
was heard in Heaven's chancery. Father Lavelle was sum-
moned to Rome, to account there for his contumacious
comments on the Archbishop, on the occasion, and would
doubtless have been imprisoned, but for the interference of
JOHN MacHALE, the great Archbishop of the West; but
the tongue of Father Lavelle, in all that relates to the political interests of Ireland, has been considerably tied ever
since. The next link in this mysterious story is furnished
by the seizure of the IRISH PEOPLE newspaper and the
imprisonment of all the gentlemen connected with it, on
the information of Nagle, the informer. Rossa, Luby,
O'Leary and several others were indicted for treason-felony
and about to take their trial when, the very week before
the trial was to take place, out comes a pastoral from Arch-

bishop Cullen, in the FREEMAN'S JOURNAL, denouncing the
untried prisoners as "revolutionists," "anarchists," "assassins," "infidels—men who would rob people of their property, and murder clergymen if they stood in their way!"
This denunciation had the desired effect; it poisoned and
excited to panic the minds of all that middle class of citizens from which juries would be formed and made up.
These prisoners were tried and condemned in the public
press, by the Irish Roman Catholic Archbishop, before they
were arraigned by the law-officers of England, in their
courts of law in Ireland! The chances for the prisoners,
from a disagreement among the jury, were cut away, and
their conviction rendered easy and certain by the early
verdict pronounced on them by the head of the Catholic
Church in Dublin! They were convicted of a "conspiracy;" and we all know how and what they suffered in the
terrible dungeons of England, and how the Catholic bishop
of Kerry, Moriarity, came out at the back of Dr. Cullen,
proclaiming that "Hell was not hot enough" nor eternity
long enough to punish these awful Fenian "infidels"
and "cut-throats." The English "interest" in Rome,
grateful for the valuable help of the Archbishop in stamping out Fenianism in Ireland, now contributed to lift the
useful Archbishop in rank over all the bishops, archbishops
and priests of Ireland. Cardinal Antonelli is again invoked,
and at last out of the Vatican comes a Cardinal's hat, with
robes of princely state, for Dr. Cullen, which gave him
rank and command and authority over every priest, bishop
and archbishop in Ireland, MacHale included. Here, again,
the "fine Roman hand" of England is apparent. The
Cardinal had thenceforth given him power to SUSPEND any
one of the hierarchy or priesthood for disobedience of his
commands—and this without appeal to Rome!

THE FENIANS IN THE FIELD.

The Fenian organization was not, however, extinguished,
either by the Cardinal's denunciations or by the state
trials, or the tortures in the British dungeons. Although

the tortures of hell were considered by His Eminence inadequate punishment for those Fenians; yet they went madly on all the same. Eighteen hundred and sixty-seven came, and with it an actual outbreak, mismanaged again, but sufficiently frightful to the English powers to displace a Tory ministry and lift to power a "reform" government, whose platform cries were "Justice to Ireland," "Ireland to be governed by Irish ideas," "tenant-right," and "equality in religion," and so on. This was a delusive platform, intended only to cajole the Fenians, who in the meantime were to be put ouside the pale of the church—were to be excommunicated—were to be refused all the sacraments of the church, living or dying, including the sacrament of matrimony; and this by an Irish bishop, an Irish cardinal, who was the son of an Irish tenant-farmer, robed in frieze and corduroy! When the great assembly of bishops was held in Rome, sometime in 1867, a movement was made in a certain chamber, in that city, between His Eminence Cullen and His Eminence Cardinal Antonelli and some other Cardinals, to get up a decree of condemnation against the Fenian Brotherhood. No sooner thought of by these Eminent princes of the Church than it was done. A bull or decree was accordingly passed through the Sacred College, condemning the Fenian Brotherhood as "a society dangerous to faith and morals," (a brief and convenient indictment) being bound by secret oaths, etc., etc., members of said organization to be refused all the sacraments until they withdrew from it; and so far as Cardinal Cullen could influence the clergy in Ireland, England and Scotland, this condemnation was carried generally into effect, as we shall see. There were many of the American bishops in Rome at that time, who, when they heard of this decree, were half crazy with rage regarding it, and wrote to their priests in America, restraining them from putting this decree in force until their return. Worse still, when the Catholic mother of Thomas Clarke Luby lay on her death bed, while her son was yet in prison for only writing in behalf of Irish independence, the rites and sacraments of her church were refused her on his account, and her body was refused sepulture in the Catholic cemetery if any persons attending her remains to the grave wore green symbols of any kind upon their persons; and the same sort of

PERSECUTIONS OF THE NATIONAL COLOR

was displayed at the great funeral of Edward Duffy to the same last resting place. To show the world how skillfully His Eminence exercises and extends his anti-Irish ideas through Ireland, in the interest of his English clients, let us contemplate the manner in which he filled up the vacancy in the See of Ossory. A chapter of the clergy of the diocese was held as usual. Three names were sent to Rome: one of these names was that of Father Moran, the Cardinal's private secretary and relative, a priest not in any manner connected with the diocese—an outsider, so to say. His Eminence had influence enough to get his secretary nominated by the Ossory convocation, whether as worthy, worthier or most worthy, none can tell; but all can see that Father Moran obtained the appointment in Rome. And it is pretty evident that this partial nomination produced the lamentable rupture between the Cardinal and Father O'Keefe. Each had a relative and favorite to canvass for. Now, His Eminence has drawn in as his secretary another clergyman, who will be, of course, a postulant for the next mitre that falls; and so on, step by step, by this method, the Irish-Catholic church and its faithful soggarths are to be West-Britonized.

"FELON-SETTING."

To show that this process of hunting down the Fenians has been undertaken by the Catholic Bishops, in conjunction with the British police, I will adduce a few indisputable facts to show that those who labored for the independence of their native Ireland, and associate for that object, no matter under what name, are to be hunted as assassins, robbers, murderers, infidels, communists, socialists, etc., and this not only by the British oligarchy, its press, its police, but by their own trusted bishops and their clergy (always with the illustrious exceptions such as the incorruptible MacHale). There was an election to be held in the County Longford, in 1869. John Martin was candidate. On the 3d of December, the Most Rev. N. MacCabe, Bishop of Longford, writing from Rome, thus spoke to his fifty priests of the Longford diocese, in a letter addressed to Rev. J. Smyth:

"As young Greville is the choice of the priests, I rely on the united efforts of priest and people to ensure his return. I have great fears lest Fenianism should get a footing in the diocese." Signed with the holy sign of the cross, by N. MacCabe. (†)

JOHN MARTIN DEFEATED.

John Martin was surely the mildest type of a Fenian, or any other man, that Ireland could produce. This Most Reverend letter-writer, however, prefers "young Greville," a captain in the British army and a lord of the Queen of England's bedchamber (whatever that may mean) to honest John Martin, whose life, labor, talents and fortune had been devoted ceaselessly to the elevation of his country. John Martin, notwithstanding his life-long services to Ireland, was defeated—defeated in a manner that will forever reflect disgrace upon this bishop and upon the clergymen who made themselves prominent leaders in the cause of the young English place-holder. At Edgeworthstown, in the County Longford, the friends of John Martin were gathered to a meeting; a procession was formed and in motion to a central point, where a large meeting of the voters was about to be held. They had banners and symbols; amongst them was a small green banner; and upon this hated banner the Rev. Father Murray—"soggarth aroon" of that parish—rushed with violent gestures, and dragging the National Flag from the hands of him who bore it, trampled it in the mud, and then waved a red pocket-handkerchief over his head!

LIFTING THE CROSS FOR ENGLAND.

Before this saddening event, the clergy of Longford, with

Father Reynolds at their head, had met at St. Mel's College to take steps respecting the Longford election. Thirty priests were present there. They raised the holy cross at that meeting, and pledged the cross and their faith and honor to vote for "young Greville," the English captain, the officer of the Queen's household, and the true representative of England in the British parliament. The aforesaid captain, subsequent to this meeting, placed £3,000 in the hands of the aforesaid soggarth Reynolds, to be used as his reverence pleased in defeating the chances of Irish independence, to which the election of honest John Martin might in some sense contribute.

THE COUNTY DRENCHED WITH WHISKY.

The money was distributed among those persons in the county who too well acted the ruffian part in that contest. Kegs of whisky and barrels of porter were let loose in every direction, and distributed, with the object of exciting the inflammable portion of these people to turn on their fellow-citizens (fellow-slaves), to drive out, to bludgeon out and to stamp out "accursed Fenianism," according to their orders. "The country was drenched with whisky," said Baron Fitzgerald, who, on solemn investigation, declared the election of the English captain void. The priests were disgraced; their religion suspected; and Ireland hung down her head. Looking outside of Ireland, we shall see what useful allies of England too often are our Irish Catholic priests. We shall see how enthusiastically THEY uphold the government of England in Ireland.

ALLIES IN AUSTRALIA

About the month of October, 1869, fifteen Fenian prisoners were released from penal servitude in Sydney, South Wales, by orders from Mr. Gladstone's Government. The Irishmen of Sydney offered these poor fellows some complimentary benefit, with a view to make up a little money to start them to some free land "where the flag of England would never more be seen." A pic-nic to a suburb of Sidney named Clontarf was proposed. But this must not be. The two chief Catholic priests of Sydney (the bishop being then at Rome), the Very Rev. S. J. A. Sheehy, V. G., and the Very Rev. John Rigney, V. G., both Irishmen,) published an injunction from the altars of all the Catholic churches in Sydney, on Sunday, November 18th, 1869, warning and commanding all Catholics to abstain from attending said pic-nic. The British government in Sydney issued also a proclamation against the holding of the meeting; but these Sydney Irishmen were not to be frightened. To the clergy, the pic-nic committee thus replied:

" We emphatically and earnestly repudiate the dictation of the Very Reverend gentlemen above, as to our meeting, which bears no religious aspect, and concerns only our rights as citizens.

[Signed]   RICHARD O'SULLIVAN,·
                                 T. O'NEIL,
                                 B. GAFFRAY,
                                 JOHN SPEVIN."

The aforesaid document will prove the existence of a semi-concordat between England and Rome, which operates far and wide, especially in the English colonies, in almost all of which the Catholic clergy are stipendiaries of the government of England.

WHO BROKE DOWN THE BRITISH CHURCH?

We will now take a second look at its operations nearer home. In the month of December, 1869, His Eminence Cardinal Cullen issued a pastoral, again condemning the Fenians, asking " What has their agitation and conspiracy produced?" He asked this question with wondrous simplicity, when it was patent, and avowed by Mr. Gladstone, Prime Minister of England, in his place in Parliament, that to " allay the Fenian excitement he had brought in his Church Bill and Land Bill "—when every newspaper in England that supported Gladstone argued that "the disturbed state of Ireland," the " Fenian conspiracy," required of the British parliament full and ample justice to allay: and John Bright, the popular member of Mr. Gladstone's

ministry, publicly declared at Birmingham, January 13th,
1870: "They would have a new invasion of Ireland with
good laws; he will astonish Ireland herself with their land
bill—one which would give the cultivators a hold of the
land which they tilled, and take away all cause for Irish
discontent and insurrection." However, this land bill was
and is the greatest kind of a delusion, as the experience of
a few short years demonstrates—witness the evictions now
going on all over Ireland and the subsequent discontent
and the " insurrection " which laid the Protestant establishment in ruins, overturned a Tory ministry and set up
he Gladstone party, and not the countless intercourse with
government of His Eminence Cardinal Cullen; and no
good measure will ever be gotten from England, except
through a " disturbance " in Ireland.

THE CARDINAL'S INFLUENCE.

The active operations of His Eminence, Cardinal Cullen,
in support of British power in Ireland are very remarkable.
Every available bishop and priest in Ireland, England and
Scotland has been seen or written to, or deputationed. Let
us contemplate the evidence to this assertion. In Kerry,
Bishop Moriarity has publicly uttered the blasphemy that
" Hell is not hot enough nor eternity long enough to sufficiently punish the Fenians." That blasphemy was uttered
some fifteen years ago, and the reverend utterer is not
gone to' h—. He performs all the sacred functions of a
Christian priest in Kerry to this day. In May, 1870, two
town councillors of Limerick waited on the acting bishop of
the diocese, Dr. Butler, at his palace in the city of Limerick
to ask his permission to make a collection at the chapel
gates, on a given day, for the families of the Fenian state
prisoners. This was refused; no Irish Fenians need apply.
Archdeacon Sullivan, of Kenmare, writing to the Dublin
NATION, April 15, 1871, boasts that in 1858 he extracted
the Phœnix revolutionary oath from one of his postulant
flock by a device which seems to the reverend gentleman
to be satisfactory to his sacerdotal conscience. Catholic

clergy are bound by their vows not to reveal anything communicated to them in the confessional. A young man had made his confession to the reverend gentleman, in the course of which he said he was a member of the Phœnix Society, and that its object was the independence of Ireland by armed insurrection. Being questioned concerning the rules of the society, he said the members were bound by oath to secrecy and obedience to their chiefs. After the interview at the confessional, the reverend gentleman took occasion to meet the young man in the street, and accosting the young man as if he, the priest, had apparently forgotten something connected with the confession, said: "By the by, what was the nature of that oath which you mentioned something about to me the other day?" The young man, thinking that he was still talking to his priest under the seal of the confessional, related to him, in the street, the nature of the Phœnix oath, which bound the members to fight for the death for Irish independence. The archdeacon, having now got out the secret IN THE STREET, sheltering his conscience by this arch device, hastened to communicate it to Dublin Castle, and actually boasted publicly that he had got there with the information before " old Trench," the magistrate; whereby the felon-setting priest "did" the felon-setting magistrate! In the well-known rising of 1867, young Colonel O'Connor, an Irish-American officer from Massachusetts, got into the southern part of Kerry, where he had rapidly organized an insurrectionary force, and was proceeding to form a junction with another body of the same kind, in a place somewhat distant. About this intended move, the Catholic priest of the district got wind, and was the first person to send a dispatch to the Government authorities respecting the intended move of the rebel colonel, which frustrated his plans. The name of this reverend gentleman I have forgotten: but he is known to many persons in Tralee, and particularly to Colonel O'Connor, who got back safely to America when all hope was lost.

THE ENGLISH CLERGY.

The Catholic clergy of England and Scotland, all the way up to and including Cardinal Manning, are dead against Ireland's independence—against all who preach such "revolutionary" doctrines. The clergy, officiating in general, take their cue from the bishops; and the English and Scotch bishops will not hear with patience a word in favor of Irish independence—will not allow any school under their control, though built, as their churches have mostly been, by the money of Irishmen, to be used for the purpose of talking even about that moderate, harmless myth known by the name of "Home Rule." Behold proof! At the Catholic chapel of Middleboro, in England, the Rev. Andrew Burns preached a sermon in May, 1870, in which he denounced the Fenians. On this occasion, some twenty or thirty of his hearers rose up and left the chapel. But the reverend gentleman went further in his denunciations than in the sermon in the chapel. He wrote a letter to the superintendent of the government works, where those who left the chapel were employed, gave their names, and denounced them as incendiaries, and unfit to be employed by the Government; and gave to the government the names of the chiefs of circles who were in their employment. Mr. John Booth, of that village, was specially denounced, though he had been all his life the most active Catholic in the parish for helping the church; and further, this Rev. Andrew Burns would not allow Booth's daughter to stand baptismal sponsor for a child which he was about to christen, because she had been to one of Mr. Meany's lectures, in the town hall, on Irish independence! At Bradford, in the same week, the Rev. Father Lacey denounced from the altar all Fenians as incendiaries, "infidels," "anarchists."

DENOUNCES THE PRESS.

He also denounced all those who read the IRISHMAN or FLAG OF IRELAND, describing their editors as "Protestant Catholics." At Newcastle-on-Tyne, Father Perrin denounced from the altar (during Mass, on January 15th, 1871), all those who sympathized with, or in any manner co-operated with the Fenian societies. He also denounced all those who sold, circulated or read the IRISHMAN or FLAG OF IRELAND. In Aberdeen, Father William Staganini preached from the altar (on Sunday, January 15th, 1871), to the congregation, on the evils of Fenianism, saying he "quite agreed with Bishop Moriarity that hell was not hot enough, nor eternity long enough for the punishment of the Fenians." He denounced to the government the members of that society in Aberdeen, threatened all such with excommunication from the church, the refusal of sacraments, etc. In York, (on January 8th, 1871, at holy mass, the Rev. Father Holland denounced the Fenians with the pains of hell, using and endorsing the blasphemies of Bishop Moriarity as to the insufficiency of hell and eternity to punish the Fenians. "There were," he said, "now residing in York certain captains and leaders of the Fenians whom he was enabled to point out, and whom he would point out to the authorities and have arrested." After the execution of the "Manchester Martyrs," this reverend gentleman said in the church, in the course of his sermon, that those "martyrs very well

DESERVED THE DEATH THEY MET WITH,

and, if any of the congregation sympathized with them, he requested them to get up and leave the church," which many of them did. Bishop Ullathorne of Salford interposed to prevent the "Irish Home Rule League" holding any of their meetings in the school-rooms which their Irish money had erected, thus driving them to the public houses. The Catholic bishop and priesthood of Glasgow interposed in like manner, prohibiting their school rooms to be used for any Irish meeting connected with the political elevation of Ireland. The Irishmen, in all those crowded places, have therefore no place to meet in but the public houses. The same rule prevails in London. We dare not open our mouths about Ireland's freedom in any of the schools attached to the Catholic churches, though those same churches and those same schools would not be in existence but for the Irish laborers of London. At the great Patrick's day demonstration in Hyde Park, last March, the Catholic clergymen refused to the Irish the use of their temperance flags for the procession. Turn which way we will, we see the hands of Catholic clerics raised against the political enfranchisement of our country. The IRISHMAN and FLAG, which uphold the right of Ireland, are excluded from the reading rooms of the "Catholic Union of Ireland," whilst the London TIMES and London PUNCH are taken in by that most exemplary society!

MORAL IN CONCLUSION.

The reader, if he have had the patience to wade through this sad history, will find in it indubitable evidence of a compact between the British Government and certain influential dignitaries of the Roman Catholic church, in Rome and Ireland, to stamp out of the Irish heart any and every aspiration for honest national government. For this purpose was the Bull against the Fenians procured at Rome : for this purpose were they excommunicated from the altars of their churches, charged with defiling with their dead the Catholic cemeteries ; their immortal souls judged—aye, judged by mortal men—and consigned to hell (with deliberate and repeated blasphemy) which it seems was not hot enough for their punishment. The British Government, taking its cue from our Cullens, our Moriaritys and our MacCabes, inflicted indescribable tortures upon the unfortunate Fenians whom they had gotten into their grasp, making them pretty nearly feel hell in their infernal dungeons. This was a new departure in the traditions and practice of the church. We never. before heard of Roman bulls issued against Irish patriots who struggled for the object the Fenians had and have in view. In 1798 Catholic priests fought in the ranks of the " Irish rebels." Father Murphy, of Wexford, the rebel general and priest, will never be blotted from the grateful memory of Irishmen :

and I might go further back, even to the times of the Kil-
kenny Confederation, 1640, when we find

POPE URBAN VIII

sending arms, ammunition and money, by his Nuncio
Renuncinni, in the frigate San Pietro, for the Irish Fenians
of that day, who had confederated to drive the English gar-
rison out of Ireland. We allege that this latter policy of
the Cullens, the Moriaritys and the rest is a departure from
the customs and traditions of the Catholic church—a
wrenching of our holy religion to the purposes of British
ascendancy—British tyranny—in our country—that the
"infidels" they speak of have been made, not by Paine
and Voltaire, but by those clergymen who cursed the
Fenians from their pulpits, refused them sacraments at their
altars, hunted them out of their churches, and marked
them out to the police for incarceration. We further say
that it has failed in its object. The whole policy and motion
and labors of the aforesaid crusaders against the Fenians
have shaken the confidence of the Irish people—Fenians
and non-Fenians—in their clergy. A terrible result; and
a heavy burden of sin on the heads of those who destroyed
this confidence.

MacHALE FORETOLD IT.

The great patriotic priest Archbishop MacHale foretold
this. He told these political bishops that "If ever the Irish
people shall withdraw their confidence from their clergy,
the fault will not be the people's" and it is now verified, as
I shall here prove in a few more lines. In the debate in
the House of Lords on the Westmeath Coercion Bill, on
May 2d, 1871, it came out that Captain Talbot, a chief of
the Irish constabulary, gave the Westmeath committee, as
a reason for his want of success in capturing Ribbonmen
and Fenians "that the Catholic clergy are now-a-days told
nothing by the people." One priest said to him: "Sometime ago I might have helped you hunt up a criminal; but
now the people do not let us know anything of their movements."

Take the recent elections as evidence to the same purport. Let the reader go with me, in memory, to the courthouse of Trim, in the county Meath, on a cold day in January, three winters ago. There is an election for a member of Parliament. The building is crowded with the candidates and their friends. One side to be proposed is Hon. J. Plunkett, son of Lord Fingal, a scion of the oldest Catholic family in Ireland, a son of the Lord Killean that was for many years the fellow-laborer of Daniel O'Connell—the best of Irish landlords, a resident Irish gentleman and all that. He had pledged himself to the Catholic priesthood to oppose Gladstone if he declined to interfere to restore the Pope to the temporal sovereignty over Rome. At his back are Father Dowling and thirty Catholic priests of the county Meath. Father Dowling rises to propose the Hon. J. Plunkett, as a fit and proper person to represent the county of Meath in the Imperial Parliament of England. The priests speech is stopped by the outburst of popular interruption which continued for an hour; and neither Father Dowling nor the Hon. Mr. Plunkett nor any one of the thirty Catholic clergymen was permitted to utter a word in that court-house, though it was filled chiefly by Roman Catholics. And now, when the High Sheriff asks for " silence," and demands to know if any other candidate is to be proposed, up stands a peasant farmer and

NOMINATES JOHN MARTIN,

our late distinguished countryman, as a fit and proper person to represent that great county in parliament—John Martin, who was not a Catholic but a frigid Presbyterian, who owned no land in the county—a convicted, transported, unrepentant " Irish rebel," who had just come down from Dublin, after unveiling the statue erected there, in the public thoroughfare, to William Smith O'Brien, another convicted rebel. What cheering then welcomed the name of John Martin in that court-house! What do those cheers for Martin tell us? " What are those wild waves saying?" Who is that audacious peasant who ventures his voice in the presence of and in opposition to the wealth of the land and the power of the priests? He must have the impudence of——William Tell. This peasant farmer is a genuine Irish patriot. The show of hands is called for. It is for Martin and Ireland's independence, and at the polls, next day, the voters roll up 1,200 votes for Martin, against 650 for the landlords and the clergy! Now that election demonstrated the mind of a large Catholic county. Those twelve hundred voters were not surely all infidels, nor assassins, nor robbers, nor Fenians; and yet they voted for Irish independence all the same, and in utter defiance too of their landlords and their clergy. It demonstrates that all the tortuous movements of the anti-Irish in Rome, in London and in Ireland have gone for nought; and, as the London TIMES remarked at that time, "Cardinal Cullen's occupation at Dublin castle is going, quite gone!" And

THIS IS GOD'S TRUTH,

though uttered by the TIMES. The county Limerick election is another case in point. On the dissolution of the last parliament by Mr. Gladstone, the Catholic clergy of Limerick met—eighty priests with their bishop, Dr. Butler, and their political mentor, Dean O'Brien. They solemnly proposed a Mr. Kelley, a Catholic landlord of the county, whose family had evicted some tenants from their lands. The Fenians proposed one of their society, who had served his due time for that cause in British dungeons,—that was his qualification in the eyes of the people of the great county Limerick—and they elected him against the active opposition of the eighty Catholic priests, the bishop, the dean and all the landlords and "respectables" of the county, three to one! Then there is

THE ELECTION OF JOHN MITCHELL,

a Protestant, a rebel, a Fenian, and even more—elected unanimously by the great Catholic county of Tipperary. If these signs and modern instances of the spirit of the Irish .

race' are not a sufficient reproof of the clerical crusades
against their freedom, more will be exhibited from day to
day, notwithstanding all the petty efforts that have been
made in Ireland to suppress the pulsations of the national
heart; notwithstanding that only one bishop in Ireland—
Most Rev. Thomas Nulty, of Meath—had the patriotism
and gratitude to attend the MacHale jubilee; notwithstanding that the students of Maynooth College are forbidden to
present him an address: notwithstanding that Cardinal
Cullen took himself off to Rome during the MacHale festi-
val, thereby showing the petty spirit that moves him—notwithstanding all this, I say, the Irish heart beats a healthy
beat for Irish Independence.

CONCLUSION IN SORROW.

This history of stupidity is written, not in malice or in a
spirit of irreligion, but in sorrow. The writer hereof and
the cardinals and the bishops will **ere** long be gathered to
their native earth. Ireland will remain; her cause will
remain and flourish, and triumph, for

> " Many a deed shall wake in praise
> That long hath slept in blame."

This narrative will form a brick in the great structure of
Irish history. It may warn future chiefs of the Catholic
church against taking sides against their country, and ad-
monish them that their faith cannot be strained and
wrenched against the independence of their country without sore injury to the faith as well as to the country.

N. T. G.

THE BULL OF ADRIAN IV.

" Adrian, bishop, servant of the servants of God, to his
dearest son in Christ, the illustrious King of England
greeting and apostolical benedictions :

" Full laudably and profitably hath your magnificence conceived the design of propagating your glorious renown on
earth, and completing your reward of eternal happiness in
heaven ; while, as a Catholic prince, you are intent on
enlarging the borders of the Church, teaching the truth of
the Christian faith to the ignorant and rude, extirpating the
roots of vice from the fields of the Lord; and, for the more
convenient execution of this purpose, requiring the counsel
and favor of the apostolic see, in which the maturer your
deliberation and the greater the discretion of your proced-
ure, by so much the happier we trust will be your progress,
with the assistance of the Lord, as all things are used to
come to a prosperous end and issue, which take their
beginning from the ardor of faith and the love of religion.

"There is indeed no doubt but that England and all the
islands on which Christ, the Sun of Righteousness hath
shone, and which have received the doctrine of the Christian faith, do belong to the jurisdiction of St. Peter and the
holy Roman church, as your excellency also doth acknowl-
edge ; and, therefore, we are the more solicitous to propagate the righteous plantation of faith in this land, and the
branch acceptable to God, as we have the secret conviction
of conscience that this is more especially our bounden
duty.   You, then, my dear son in Christ, have signified to
us your desire to enter into the island of Ireland, in order
to reduce the island to obedience under the laws, and to
extirpate the plants of vice ; and that you are willing to
pay from each a yearly pension of one penny to St. Peter,
and that you will preserve the rights of the churches of this
land whole and inviolate.   We, therefore, with that grace

and acceptance suited to your pious and laudable design, and favorably assenting to your petition, do hold it good and acceptable that, for extending the borders of the Church, restraining the progress of vice, for the correction of manners, the planting of virtue and the increase of religion, you enter the island, and execute therein whatever shall pertain to the honor of God and welfare of the land; and that the people of this land receive you honorably, and reverence you as their lord, the rights of their churches still remaining sacred and inviolate and saving to St. Peter the annual pension of one penny from every house.

"If then you be resolved to carry the design you have conceived into effectual execution, study to form this nation to virtue and manners, and labor by yourself and others you shall judge meet for this work, in faith, word and life, that the Church may be there adorned, that the religion of the Christian faith may be planted and grow up, and that salvation of souls be so ordered, that you may be entitled to the fullness of heavenly reward from God, and obtain a glorious renown on earth throughout all ages. Given at Rome in the year of salvation, 1166."

(O'Halloran Hist. of Ireland, page 305.)

England has always acted from self-interest. She has at all times endeavored rather to change the mode of persecution than to desist from worrying her victim. * * Ireland, rich in soil and blooming in culture, was made a prey to every species of tyrany and despotism, until her fertile plains resembled a charnel house from the executioner. * * In short, the annals of the world exhibit no parallel to the cruelty and perfidy by which England established her power in Ireland.

BISHOP ENGLAND.

No government, whether Christian, Mohamedan or Pagan, was ever sullied with more crime, or marked with more utter baseness, adroit diplomacy, low intrique, base selfish-

ness, insatiate rapacity, open treachery, high-handed spolia-
tion and robbery. Cold-blooded cruelty and persecution,
and downright butchery have ever marked the policy of
of England toward Ireland.

ARCHBISHOP SPAULDING.

Martial law for the people, gold for the senate, a bayonet
for the patriot who loved Ireland, and a bribe for the traitor
who did not.

ARCHB'P HUGHES.

The King of England, finding himself unable to reduce
Ireland by force of arms, had resource to every stratagem,
even to religion, to conquer this kingdom.

Westmonasteriensir says that he solicited, through a solemn
embassy, the new Pope Adrian, (confident of obtaining it
of him, as he was an Englishman) for leave to enter Ireland
in a hostile manner, to subjugate it. It is alleged, that he
represented to him that religion was almost extinct in the
country, that the morals of the people were corrupted, and
that it was necessary to remedy it, for the glory of Christianity.

In his zeal he offered to become an apostle for that end,
on condition that his holiness would grand him the sovereignty of the island, and also promised to pay Peter's pence
for every house. The Pope, who was born his subject,
readily granted him (Henry) his request; and the liberty of
an entire nation was sacrificed to the ambition of one
through the complaisance of the other. Like an able states-
man, Henry wanted a favorable opportunity to carry his
project into execution. This presented itself in a civil war
that broke out between the monarch and the king of Leinster, of which he took advantage to begin his mission; and
although, according to the law of God, it is not by dispoiling
our neighbor of his property that we should convert him,
still the missionaries whom Henry II employed were men
with arms in their hands, and more intent upon converting

the land to their own use, to the predjudice of the old proprietors, than gaining souls to God.

(McGoeghegan and Mitchell's History of Ireland, p. 257, Chap. XVI.

AUTHORITIES ON THE BULLS.

If it should be enquired in this place upon what account Diarmuid, king of Leinster, chose to commit himself and his affairs under the protection of the king of England, rather than to the king of France, it must be understood that Donough, the son of Byron Borroimhe, was a prince very unacceptable to the principle nobility of Ireland, who, rather than pay obedience, unanimously came to a revolution to make a present of the whole island to Urbanus II, pope of Rome, which was done in the year of our redemption, 1092 : so that by this donation the popes laid claim to the sovereignty of Ireland, which they executed so far as to govern the nobility and clergy by wholesome laws, and to establish a regular discipline in the church. And the Popes maintained this authority till Adrian, the fourth of that name, sat in St. Peter's chair, which was in the year of our Lord, 1154. This pope was an Englishman by descent, and his original name was Nicholas Brusber, or Breakspeire.

Stone, the English annalist, asserts in his chronicle, that this pope bestowed the Kingdom of Ireland upon Henry II in the first year of his reign and Anno Domini, 1154.

He also relates, that this donation was conferred upon the king, on condition that he would revive the profession of the Christian faith, which was dead throughout the Island ; that he should polish (?) the rude manners of the people, (?) defend and restore the rights and revenues of the church and clergy, and take especial care that every inhabited house in the kingdom should pay annually one penny to the Pope, under the name of St. Peter's penny.

This grant of the Kingdom of Ireland to Henry, was drawn up in writing, which, when he received, he sent John, bishop of Salisbury, with this instrument of the Pope's donation into Ireland. Upon his landing at Waterford, he sent to the bishops and the principle clergy of the island, and gave them an account of his commission.

They attended upon him at Waterford, when he published the pope's grant of the Kingdom of Ireland to Henry the II, King of England, with the conditions to be performed on his part, and by all who succeeded in that crown. The clergy took the matter into consideration, and after some debate an instrument was drawn up, which contained their absolute submission to this donation of the Pope, and to this they all unanimously subscribed.

The bishop returned with this confirmation of the Pope's grant by the clergy of Ireland, and the king of England sent the same prelate with the instrument to the Pope, who was well pleased with the submission of the Irish clergy, and sent a ring to king Henry as a confirmation of his former grant, by which he was established in the possession of the Irish Crown.

Bellarmine, an eminent cardinal, agrees with this account. In a part of his work are these words : "Adrian IV, Pope "of Rome, by birth an Englishman, a wise and pious man, "hath granted the island of Ireland to Henry II, king of "England, upon condition that he propagates virtues in "that island, and extirpates vice ; that he takes care that "one penny be paid yearly to St. Peter by every house, "and that he preserves the rights of the church inviolable : "the diploma is extant in the 12th volume of Cardinal "Baronius."

Stanehurst, in his chronicle, asserts the same thing, where he gives the account that Henry II, king of England, procured a bull from Adrian, Pope of Rome, which enjoined the clergy of Ireland, and likewise the nobility of the kingdom, to pay obedience to Henry II, upon the conditions and under the restrictions herein contained. The same

author likewise relates, that Alexander III sent a cardinal
(whose name was Vivian) into Ireland, to inform the subjects of that kingdom to the grant that he and the prece-
dent Pope made that kingdom to Henry II, king of England, by the tenor of which that crown was confirmed to
Henry and his successors in St. Peter's chair, a yearly
tribute of a penny from every house throughout the Island.

It appears therefore, that the reasons why Diarmuid, king
of Leinster, applied to the king of England rather than any
other prince, was because the king of England laid claim to
the kingdom of Ireland, by virtue of the donation from the
popes above mentioned ; and therefore that king had power,
by his superior authority, to adjust the pretences of the
princes of Ireland, and to engage in their disputes, and con-
sequently to interpose in the quarrels of the king of Leinster,
and settle him in the possession of that province."

(Butler's History of Ireland, p. 301-305.)

Adrian IV. the Pontiff, who authorized Henry of England
to annex Ireland to his crown, died by swallowing a fly in
a cup of water.

(Walsh's Eccles. History of Ireland, p. 109.)

Pope Adrian, the Fourth, in the second year of his Pontificate 1155, granted to Henry the Second, of Ireland, a
bull, authorizing the invasion of Ireland. The authenticity
of that bull is now universally admitted.

(T. D. McGee's History of Ireland, p. 136, Chap. 4, Book
3, Vol. 1.)

The Irish princes did not act, unfortunately, that independent part which became men who lived in this crisis of
their country's affairs. Divided among themselves, and
submissive to the ordinances of the church, while we revere
their feelings a Christians, we cannot but deplore their conduct and tame submission as freemen.

(Mooney's History of Ireland, p. 564.)

NOTE. - T. Mooney's lectures, called Irish History, written in 1845, under the aus-
pices of the clergy of New York, and others, he only casts doubt on the bull, but
confesses they were read at the synod of Cashel. (See page 561.)

THE LETTERS

OF

Niall the Grand and Others,

ON

IRISH HISTORY.

BULLS OF ADRIAN, ETC., ETC.

Dedicated to the Fenians and the Friends of Ireland.

"Semper et Ubique Fideles."—Always and Everywhere Faithful.

SECOND EDITION--REVISED,

COPYRIGHT SECURED.

GRAND RAPIDS, MICH.:
STEAM PRESSES OF H. H. COLESTOCK, 2 PEARL STREET.
1882.

www.ingramcontent.com/pod-product-compliance
Lightning Source LLC
Chambersburg PA
CBHW022010050726
47499CB00008BA/2817